Death in the Cards

A Willows Bend Cozy Mystery Book 3

Evelyn Cullet

Evelyn Cullet

Published by Evelyn Cullet

ISBN 979-8-218-22990-0

Typesetting services by BOOKOW.COM

*In fond memory of my brother-in-law, Adam Chwajol, a master practitioner of *Cartomancy.*

*Cartomancy: The age old art of reading playing cards.

Acknowledgments

Editor: Erynn Newman, A Little Red Ink.

Book Cover Design: 100 Covers

Chapter 1

A loud, continuous knocking on her front door startled Heather Stanton out of her daydreams of becoming a successful marketing executive once again. She jumped off the kitchen stool where she'd spent the last two hours working at her laptop.

Aunt Julia sat forward on the living room sofa in their cozy new apartment, hovering over several open books on the occult spread across the coffee table. "Who could that be at nine o'clock on a Saturday night?"

Heather and her aunt had only lived in Willows Bend a few weeks, and they didn't know many people. The last time she opened the front door to a stranger, it turned out to be a disaster. Grabbing the pepper-spray from her purse, Heather slipped it into her jeans pocket. At least she'd be prepared this time.

She leaned into the door. "Who is it?"

"It's me," a familiar, but unwelcome, baritone voice answered.

Heather's heart raced as heat rose to her face.

"It can't be." She opened the door a crack, took a peek, and slammed it shut. "Aunt Julia, when you said it would only be a matter of time before something bad happened, you were right."

The knocking continued, and the voice called out, "Open the door, Heather. I just want to talk to you."

Julia closed her book. "Who is it?"

Heather could barely get the name out. "Ja… Jack Steele."

The older woman's graying eyebrows arched as her large brown eyes gazed into Heather's. "Your ex? I don't blame you for not answering it. Do you want me to get rid of him?" She pushed herself off the sofa and slid her feet into a pair of light blue scuffs. "I'll get my baseball bat."

Heather put a hand up to stop her. "No, I can handle it."

Every time Aunt Julia grabs her bat, calamity strikes, and I'm in no mood for that kind of trouble tonight.

"Suit yourself." Julia plopped down on the sofa and picked up one of the occult books.

Heather hated confrontations. Her thoughts became jumbled, heat burned her cheeks, and her knees always turned to mush.

Determined to appear cool this time, she squared her shoulders, focused on good thoughts, and straightened her backbone. Taking a deep breath to relieve the tightness in her chest, she ran tense fingers through her long, auburn hair, and swung the door open.

Jack Steele leaned against the door jamb, his sandy hair lay fringed across his forehead and his slate-gray eyes crinkled in amusement. "Hi, Sweetheart."

He gave her that half-smile meant to melt her heart. And it did at one time, but now she realized it was just the satisfied smirk of a man whose ego knew no bounds.

"How are you?" He used the deep velvety tone he put on to seduce women, herself included.

Heather clenched her teeth, trying to get past his phony concern. "I'm good. What do you want?"

Slipping a hand into his designer jeans pocket to appear casually at ease, Jack glanced around. "What, no welcome? Aren't you going to invite me in?"

"No." Heather stepped out of the doorway into the brightly lit, carpeted stair landing and closed the door behind her as she breathed in the familiar scent of his expensive, potent cologne.

There was no way the scent of Amouage was invading her apartment again. Not after she'd just spent days getting rid of it from that little stunt he pulled on her last week, when he'd forwarded all her clothes, soaked in the fragrance.

A fake frown pulled his thin lips downward. "And after I came all the way from Chicago to this jerkwater town to see you. Why won't you take my phone calls or respond to my texts and emails?"

She crossed her arms, ignoring his question. This time she couldn't curb the anger in her voice. "I'll only ask you one more time. What do you want?"

"I want to talk." His eyes scanned the white hallway walls and the faux glass light fixture overhead. "But not here. Let's go someplace where we can have a drink like civilized human beings. How about the Franklin House hotel bar?"

While the hotel was the only place to stay here in town, she didn't need to be seen with her ex-boyfriend in the bar. That would set tongues wagging. Willows Bend was a small town, and like all small towns, gossip spread like wild fire.

"If you want to talk, we can talk right here. If not, you can leave."

Jack put his fists on his hips. "You've got to be kidding."

Heather perched on the top step.

He looked down at her, a posture she was used to when she was with him. Then he heaved a sigh and sat down next to her. "All right, if those are your terms."

This was a surprise. He rarely, if ever, gave in to her. And usually then, only to get what he wanted. So, he must want something.

They sat in momentary silence.

Heather waved a hand in front of her face to push the Amouage scent away. It was more than she could cope with right now. Then she folded her arms across her heart. *He's not going to get to me this time.*

"What do you want to talk about?" She tried to sound casual.

He raised one eyebrow, squinted his other eye, and flattened his lips. This was the look he used when he was getting right to the point.

"I'll get right to the point," he said.

She pressed her lips together to suppress a laugh.

Jack leaned in close. "I'd like to know why you unceremoniously dumped me? The least you can do is give me an explanation."

So that's it? He's looking for closure. The man was unbelievable. After catching him *in flagrante* with another woman, she'd packed a bag, grabbed her laptop, and left his swanky, downtown Chicago condo forever. And *he* needed an explanation?

"How can you ask me that, after what I saw you doing in our bedroom with...whatever her name was?"

His eyes took on that phony sincere look she'd come to recognize so well. "It wasn't what you think. It meant nothing. She was just a client who needed comforting."

Where have I heard that before? They were all beautiful, lonely clients whose divorces he'd just handled, looking for sympathy and a shoulder to cry on from their handsome lawyer. And his was always so convenient. Well, she'd had enough. He wasn't going to gaslight her again with one of his manipulative explanations about how what she saw was not what was really happening. Not when lying came as easy to him as breathing.

Even though losing wasn't one of Jack's strong points, she had to convince him she no longer cared. This wouldn't be easy. He was a much stronger litigator than she could ever be.

Heather put a hand to her forehead. "There's nothing to talk about. Why can't you just accept the fact that we're through... done... finished? We are no longer a couple. There's nothing left to say."

Jack's gray eyes stared into hers. "I have plenty to say, if you'll just give me the chance." His voice was soft and sincere, and she felt herself weakening.

Then, remembering all he'd done to her, she found a sudden moment of strength. "I don't want to hear any more. Goodbye!"

She got up, went into her apartment, and slammed the door in his face.

Heather hated being mean to anyone, but she didn't know how else to rid herself of Jack. He'd talked her into taking him back so many times only to resume his old habits. And what was worse, his loyal friends always covered for him.

She locked the door. "Never again!"

Julia looked up from the book she was reading. "Is he gone?"

Heather wiped the perspiration from her upper lip. "For good, I hope."

"You look tense," Julia said. "What did I tell you about scrunching up your face like that?"

Scrunching when she was upset made her emotions so easily readable. But it was a habit Heather found hard to break.

Julia went to the kitchen and poured two fingers of Crown Royal into a juice glass. She handed it to her niece. "Drink this."

Whiskey wasn't her drink of choice, but since it was the only alcohol in the apartment, Heather gulped it, sputtered, and coughed. Within a few moments, it eased her tense shoulders and calmed her hectic breathing. She set the glass in the sink.

"Thanks. I needed that."

There were times her aunt knew exactly what to say and do to make her feel better. And then, there were other times when Julia frustrated the heck out of her, but she didn't want to think about those times right now.

Julia went to the living room and plopped on the sofa with the remote. "I'll turn on the TV and see if there's anything you can watch to take your mind off things."

Heather wouldn't be able to keep her thoughts on a TV program, not when her exchange with Jack was playing on repeat in her mind. She hoped her cold, indifference worked, and he'd leave her alone. But she couldn't shake the little voice at the back of her mind that told her bad repercussions might still happen if she pushed him too far. She'd already experienced what his anger could do—some of her clothes still reeked of Amouage.

She grabbed a jelly donut from the counter and bit into it as she paced the kitchen floor in an effort to walk off her frustration.

Julia strolled into the kitchen, dug into her purse, and pulled out a deck of playing cards. "Well, if you don't want to watch television, then let's see what your future holds."

Chapter 2

"YOU'RE going to tell my fortune with playing cards?" Heather never believed in fortune telling. "Thanks, but I'll pass."

Julia shuffled the cards. "If *you're* not interested, I'll see what *my* future holds."

A text message from Chad Willows, their landlord, and Heather's current love interest came up on her cell phone. She let out a sigh of relief that she didn't have to deal with her aunt's fortune telling, or with Jack the Zipper Ripper, again tonight.

Heather read the text aloud. "Interested in temp job? Meet me at The Athena at 11:00 a.m. tomorrow."

A temporary job? Thank goodness. And just in time. Money was in short supply these days without steady work. She hoped she wouldn't have to sell what little jewelry she had left to pay her part of next month's rent.

"The Athena," she read again.

Heather had been to the classy restaurant once before on a date-slash-clue-finding-mission when her aunt had been suspected of murder.

Julia laid some cards on the coffee table. "Isn't that the place the mayor financed with his horse race winnings?"

If anyone knew about betting on horses, it was her aunt, who was addicted to it, although Julia considered it more of a predilection for horses than an addiction to gambling.

"Yes," Heather said. "But from what I hear, that was a long time ago, and he wasn't the mayor then."

A grunt emanated from Julia's throat as she studied the cards. "This isn't good."

"What's the matter?" Don't you think I should take the job I'm offered?"

Julia glanced up, and her eyes flashed. "I just laid out two aces and two eights in clubs and spades."

"What does that mean?"

"It's the hand Wild Bill Hickok was holding when he was shot dead at a poker table. And ever since, it's been known as the *dead man's hand*, an omen of bad things to come."

"So it's just another superstition."

"Call it what you will, but I see death in the cards." Julia picked them up one by one. "Maybe I'm interpreting them wrong, but whatever they're trying to tell me looks ominous. I'll try again tomorrow morning."

She dropped her shoulders and let out a sigh as if she knew the result wouldn't change. "I do think you should take the job if you want it, but if you don't, put in a good word for me."

Heather poured hot water into her cup and then dropped in a chamomile tea bag. "You have your hands full with community service every weekday for the next several months. Wouldn't adding a job on top of that be a little too much?"

Julia slipped the deck of cards back into its box. "You're right. I can't work seven days a week. When would I have time to rid myself of this horrible curse? It must be what the cards are warning me about."

Heather couldn't stop Julia from raging on about that mythical curse some old crone had cast on her for refusing to marry her son, so he could remain in the country. Her aunt said she'd tried just about every ritual in all the occult books she could find, and she still hadn't gotten rid of it, even though nothing bad had happened to them in the last couple of weeks, except for Jack pouring his cologne all over Heather's clothes and then showing up tonight. But he was *her* curse, not her aunt's.

Julia patted the sofa cushion next to her for Heather to sit. "Looks like there are some good old reruns on."

Heather set her mug and half-eaten donut on the coffee table. She was still uneasy about her encounter with Jack. *If Chad and I had been on a date, there would have been no doubt in Jack's mind that I was over him.* She sighed. *What a waste of a perfectly good Saturday night.*

She'd hoped, by now, after everything that had happened between them in the past couple of weeks, Chad Willows, ex P.I. and bookstore owner, had developed some real feelings for her. He'd complimented her on several occasions, but he seemed reluctant to ask her out, and she didn't know why.

Of course, now that he'd probably heard her ex was back in town, their romance would be next to impossible to rekindle, if there was any spark to begin with on his part. She shoved the last of the donut into her mouth in an effort to make herself feel better.

<><><>

On Sunday morning, Heather checked the weather. Sunny and in the upper 80s. Another hot day, and it was just the first week of June.

Rummaging through her closet, she pulled out her favorite pale green, sleeveless, Tribeca mini-dress. It flattered her figure and brought out the emerald green of her eyes. Then she slipped into a pair of white Alexander McQueen strappy sandals and straightened her long, auburn hair. The look had always made an impression in the past, and she hoped it would work with Chad.

After applying her makeup, she grabbed the matching white clutch bag and bid her aunt goodbye. But when she opened the door, she nearly tripped over Jack, who was sitting on the top step in the hallway just outside their apartment. He shot to his feet and brushed the wrinkles out of his white polo shirt and beige Bermuda shorts. She wanted to turn around and go back in, but she couldn't be late for that appointment with Chad.

"What are you doing here?"

He put his hands up as though he was trying to fend her off. "I know you told me we were through last night, and I've accepted it. Well… I almost have. But I really need to talk to you about something else. It's important."

Should I give him the benefit of the doubt? She'd done it before and had been sorry, but this time his attitude was different, although she couldn't put her finger on why.

She checked the time on her cell phone. "Okay, but I can't talk now. I'm late for an important... um... date."

He eyed her clothes. "So that's why you look so gorgeous this morning. I'm jealous. Who's the lucky guy?"

She ignored his question and rushed past him down the stairs. "I don't want to be late. I'll call you when I'm free."

He followed her out the door. "What am I supposed to do while I'm waiting?"

Once they were on the sidewalk, Heather hitched her thumb toward a small, square sign hanging on the corner lamp post. It had a silhouette of a horse's head with the initials OTB inside a white arrow pointing east.

"There's an off-track betting facility about three blocks from here. Just follow the signs." In her peripheral vision, she spotted the familiar figure of Johnny Tanner, the accountant who worked there, jogging in that direction. "If you follow that man," She jutted her chin after him, "he'll lead you right to it. That should keep you busy for the day. I'll call you... later." Which she had no intention of doing.

She slipped her sunglasses on and drove her blue Chevy rental toward The Athena. It was the only upscale eating establishment in the small town of Willows Bend. Constructed of white brick and glass, it gave the area a much-needed upgrade. And it was conveniently located not far from the apartment she shared with her aunt above the *Willow in the Wind Bookstore,* which just happened to be owned by Chad Willows and his sister, Ashley.

As she drove through downtown Willows Bend, the eclectic assortment of quaint boutiques situated on tree-lined streets pushed Jack and his problems out of her mind.

Once she parked her car in the restaurant lot, the queasiness began. It had been a few years since she'd gone to a job interview, if that's what this was, and nerves had gotten to her before. Plus, she had no idea what this job might entail or even if she was qualified.

Heather checked her face and hair in the rear-view mirror before getting out of the car. At the front of the restaurant, she adjusted her dress before pushing the door open. The cool air gave her bare arms goose bumps. *Maybe wearing a sleeveless dress wasn't such a good idea.*

A young man with curly, sun-bleached hair, dressed in a black and white uniform, greeted her with a smile. "Good morning. Welcome to *The Athena*. Do you have a reservation?"

"Oh, I'm not sure. I'm meeting someone, so I'll wait here if you don't mind?"

He raised his eyebrows. "Not at all."

A moment later, Chad strolled up to her, his sky-blue eyes shining. "Hi Heather. I'm glad you came. You look beautiful."

She couldn't help smiling back at his handsome face as her skin warmed to the point where she could no longer feel the air conditioning. "Thanks."

He looked amazing in his white linen shirt and tan dress pants. But then, he'd look great in anything with his six-foot-one athletic build.

She glanced around. "You said something about a job opportunity?"

"I wasn't sure if you'd still be interested, since your boyfriend's in town."

"Jack Steele is not my boyfriend any longer, and he never will be again."

Chad nodded. "I remember you telling me about him. He came in the bookstore yesterday afternoon, questioning us about you. He didn't even recognize me, and I worked as a P.I. for one of his law partners in Chicago until a month ago. By the way he talked, he seemed pretty confident about winning you back."

She'd been trying to get Chad to ask her out for weeks, and now he thinks she's rekindling a relationship with her old boyfriend. She wasn't about to let Jack take one more thing from her.

"We've been broken up for weeks, since I caught him cheating, but yesterday I made sure he knew we were over once and for all." She smiled, hoping it would get Chad to stop talking about it. "Please, tell me why I'm here."

He led her through the austere restaurant teeming with customers seated at small, rectangular tables that were located much too close together.

A section at the back was partitioned off by a five-foot-high white trellis, enclosed on three sides. Inside was a large, round table with six gleaming place settings. A crystal vase of colorful wild flowers had been made into an attractive centerpiece. Oak chairs with burgundy seats occupied each setting.

"This is lovely."

Maybe the job offer was only a ruse. As much as she wanted to be on a date with Chad, she hoped it wasn't, because what she really needed right now was a steady income.

She started to ask him about the job, when a short, stout man in a beige suit stalked up to the table, cell phone in hand.

Chad turned to face him. "Mayor Bandik, this is—"

Before Chad could finish, the mayor grabbed Heather's hand in his bear paw and pumped her arm. "You don't have to tell me who this lovely lady is. She and her aunt have been all over the local news lately."

Heather cringed. *I hope a little involvement in a couple of murder investigations doesn't negatively affect my chances of getting the job.*

The mayor's pale brown eyes searched hers. "I've been looking forward to meeting you, Miss Stanton. I must commend you on working with the police to rid this town of those undesirables." He released her hand.

Whew! "Thank you." She didn't know what else to say, surprised he was so informal about it all. Then she looked past the mayor at the short man who came rushing toward him.

The mayor glanced over his shoulder. "This is my accountant, Marty Engels."

Marty's small, beady eyes, behind overly large, horn-rimmed glasses, searched the room and finally rested on Heather. A drop of sweat dripped down his forehead, and he wiped it away with a handkerchief. "Pleased to meet you."

She smiled and shook his outstretched, moist hand. After he released hers, she searched the area for something to wipe it with, but there was nothing except the cloth napkin on the table next to her. She'd just have to wait.

"So, Miss Stanton," the mayor continued. "Chad tells me you're looking for a temporary job, just until your aunt's community service has been completed."

"That's right. I am." She didn't want to sound too desperate, so she added, "Actually, I'm starting my own online marketing business, but until it's up and running, I could use the extra income."

A wide smile blazed across the mayor's chubby face. "You sound like a real go-getter. Good. I created a position for you within my staff. Be at my office in City Hall..." He flipped through several screens on his cell phone and studied the final one a moment before looking up. "At 10:15 tomorrow morning, and I'll give you the details."

He turned to leave, then stopped and pivoted back. "Oh, one more thing, Miss Stanton. Email your resume to my office sometime today." He handed her a card with his information on it, then raised his hand. "Just a formality, you understand."

She nodded. "Of course."

"Then I'll see you tomorrow morning." He flipped a hand toward the empty table. "Why don't you two stay for lunch? My treat." He smiled his goodbye and was gone as quickly as he had appeared, trailed by his wimpy-looking accountant.

Stunned, Heather stood with her mouth open, unable to say anything. "That was… overwhelming."

"Yeah, he's got a strong personality. That's from being in politics, but he's been a good mayor for many years."

She waited for Chad to say something about the job or about lunch. When he didn't, she asked, "Do you have any idea what this job entails?"

He shook his head. "I don't have a clue."

"Well then, are we having lunch?"

He checked his cell phone. "Sorry, I can't. I have to pick up Ashley and open the bookstore at noon. We do our best business on the weekends when the train brings in out-of-town shoppers. But you can stay, if you want. Or call, I don't know... someone *else* to join you."

Chad knew she didn't have any real friends in town yet. *Two can play that game.* "Maybe I will call *someone*. Someone who would appreciate my company."

She could have kicked herself as soon as the words left her mouth. *Why did I say that?* Maybe she was being a little too sensitive where Chad was concerned.

He grunted. "Good luck with the new job. I hope it's something you're not *overqualified* for."

Heat rose to her cheeks. They'd had this conversation before when she'd told him that with her education, she thought she was overqualified to be a retail clerk. He didn't take that well since his business was retail. *At this rate, our romance will never get off the ground.*

She should have said something to let him know she wasn't serious, but she couldn't catch him before he rushed out the door. And if she texted him, she'd only seem desperate.

Heather pulled a chair from under the table, eased herself into it, and wiped the accountant's perspiration from her hand on the napkin at the place setting.

A middle-aged waiter came to the table. "May I take your drink orders?"

"I won't be having a drink, and Mr. Willows had to leave, but I'd like to order two crab salads to go."

"Your order will be ready for pick up at the bar in about ten minutes."

"Thanks."

She tapped her Aunt Julia's contact on her cell. When she answered, Heather said, "Don't make lunch."

"I was just about to call you." Julia's voice shook, like she was nervous or frightened. "I think you'd better come home right away."

Heather tried not to sound suspicious. "Why?"

"You'll find out when you get here."

Heather stared at her phone. *What has Aunt Julia done now?*

Chapter 3

ALL sorts of unimaginable things crossed Heather's mind on the way home. She took the stairs two at a time and unlocked the apartment door. Rushing inside, she found her aunt leaning against the back wall next to the door, wide-eyed and holding her aluminum baseball bat as if she was getting ready to hit someone with it.

"I was in the living room when I heard a creaking noise coming from the back stairs," Julia said. "And then it sounded like someone was snooping around the back door, so I went to get my bat."

Breathless, Heather dropped her shoulders. *Is that all?* She set the take-out bag on the counter.

"It was probably just Chad going upstairs to the attic to look through his grandfather's things. He told me he hasn't done anything with them since he passed away several months ago."

"Oh." Julia blinked a few times as she set her bat on the floor. "That must have been it."

When her aunt was so willing to agree, it left a huge question in Heather's mind. Julia was always the first to argue a point.

"Have you heard footsteps on the back landing before?" Heather asked.

"Yes, just about every night this week. But I thought it was my imagination getting the better of me. Ever since I started working with the occult books, I've been imagining all kinds of... things."

Red flag. Heather pulled out two containers of crab salad from the take-out bag. "What kind of things?"

Julia opened a container and inspected the food inside. "Looks delicious."

Evasive was her aunt's favorite kind of answer.

Heather hopped onto one of the kitchen stools at the counter and opened her container. "It's strange that I haven't heard any footsteps."

Julia grabbed a fork and took an experimental taste. "Mmm. This is yummy." She stirred the contents of the container. "I occasionally have these nightmares about demons and gargoyles watching and waiting for some kind of signal from Beelzebub to do..." She shrugged one shoulder. "Whatever evil they do. Maybe I just dreamt I heard footsteps. That might explain the eerie light I thought I saw under the back door the other night."

Heather nearly choked on her salad. She swallowed hard to clear her throat. "Have you been sleepwalking again?"

Julia lifted a forkful of salad. "I don't think so, but then, I wouldn't know if I was, would I?"

This disturbed Heather. Something needed to be done before things got out of hand. If having these scary dreams caused Julia to start sleepwalking again, there was no telling where she might end up, or who she may meet on the back stairs in the middle of the night.

"I think you should see someone about your problem."

"I don't know what you mean." Julia folded her arms across her ample chest. "What problem?"

"The nightmares and the possible sleepwalking." Without finishing her lunch, Heather climbed off the stool and went to her laptop. She was about to search for the nearest psychiatric practice but stopped with her hands in mid-air. "Do you have medical insurance or any money saved to see a doctor who could help you?"

Julia hesitated. "Not right now. I have just enough to cover rent and food. Insurance will have to wait. My horses haven't been coming in lately. And that evil curse is the cause of it."

Heather closed her eyes and tried to calm the aggravation building up inside. "You can't blame every bad thing that happens to you on that stupid curse. Bad things happen to everyone. Sometimes we have no control over them."

"Yeah, well... we'll see."

Heather was tired of arguing about the curse. It wouldn't do any good. She'd try another tactic to convince Julia the evil curse was all in her mind. "You told me you didn't need luck when it came to betting on the horses, because you had know-how."

Heather was astounded at the words that came out of her mouth. It sounded like she was supporting her aunt's gambling habit instead of convincing her to quit. Or maybe she'd finally accepted it as a part of her aunt's personality.

"It seems my natural gift is out of sync because it's struggling against the curse, which is probably why my horses haven't been in the mood to win."

Heather's annoyance with her aunt had built up to the point where she had to let it out in one long breath.

There was no arguing with Julia's logic since she didn't understand it, anyway. Time to try something else.

"I'll call Chad and ask him if he's been climbing up to the attic lately. That should put your mind at ease about demons and gargoyles hovering around on our back landing."

"Wait." Julia picked up her occult books and shoved them into a plastic bag. "I'll ask him myself. I have to go downstairs and return these books I bought last week."

"I thought you'd gotten some good rituals from those books."

"They had the wrong kind of rituals, not what I was looking for. So I'm returning them."

"I'll go with you. I need to talk to Chad." *To explain what I said at the restaurant, before he starts believing it's true.*

<><><>

As they walked out the street door, an ambulance, siren screaming, sped to the alley behind the store and stopped. It was followed by a black and white police car with two officers inside. Heather and Julia strained their necks in an effort to see what was going on, but officer Sam Henderson got out and held them back.

"What happened?" Heather asked.

"Krystal Stamos was out jogging and found a man lying in the alley behind the bookstore at the foot of your back staircase."

Why was Chad's ex-fiancée jogging around here on a hot Sunday morning?

An image of the tall, slim, former underwear model wearing short-shorts and a tank top crossed Heather's mind.

Julia shifted from foot to foot with her eyes wide. "Who is he?"

"Don't know yet," Officer Henderson answered.

"What happened to him?" Heather asked.

"Don't know that either. But I'm sure it'll be on the local news station sometime today." The officer pointed to the corner where the news van had just pulled up.

Heather didn't want to be on the news again. It might jeopardize the job at city hall. "Well, I hope he's okay." She grabbed Julia's arm and nudged her toward the bookstore.

The tinkle of the bell on the door had Chad's sister Ashley glancing in their direction as she sat in her wheelchair at the window, changing the book display. Makkie, her sleek black cat, sat next to her looking, for all intents and purposes, like a statue with bright green eyes.

He meowed and jumped down to greet them.

Julia shuddered and veered away from him, setting her book bag on the front counter. "I'd like to return these books."

Her aunt was not fond of Makkie due to past differences.

Heather smiled and stooped down to pet his smooth, silky fur. She adored the loveable feline.

"Okay." Ashley wheeled her motorized chair down the aisle toward the front counter. "I'll be right there."

Her shoulder-length, jet black hair was pulled into a ponytail, tied with a pink ribbon, the same color as the short-sleeved, breezy blouse she wore over white skinny jeans. Makkie trotted behind her, tail swishing from side to side.

"What's all the commotion in the alley?" Ashley scanned the books and handed Julia back the money she'd collected from her last week.

"Don't you know?" Julia asked.

"No. My brother just went out to see."

"According to Officer Henderson," Heather said. "Krystal Stamos found a man lying at the bottom of the back stairs sometime this morning, while she was jogging past. They have no details yet."

Julia harrumphed as she made her way to the occult section of the store.

Ashley turned her wheelchair around. "Guess I'll wait for Chad to come back. If anyone can get information out the police, he can. He and Sam Henderson have known each other since elementary school."

Heather wanted to ask Ashley if it was Krystal's habit to jog around this neighborhood on a Sunday but thought better of it. Instead, she headed to the back door to check if the news cameras where filming. She and her aunt had been mixed up in three murder investigations, and she didn't want to get involved in another one.

Ashley wheeled over to Heather. "What did you do to my easy-going, even-tempered brother?"

Heather gazed at the floor. "I don't think I did anything to him."

"Well, you must have either said or done something, because he's really edgy this morning, and he seldom looses his temper unless there's a very good reason. Ever since he opened the store today, he's been pacing the floor and mumbling to himself. He's even snapped at me a few times."

Heather shrugged. "What makes you think I'm the cause of it?"

Ashley widened her eyes. "He told me he was going to meet you at The Athena. You must have said something to upset him. Haven't you noticed the way he looks at you?"

Julia stuck her head around a bookcase and called out, "I have."

Heather didn't know what to think, but in her heart, she hoped it was true. "If he likes me so much, then why hasn't he asked me out?"

Ashley waved a hand as if to dismiss Heather's words. "He's got some crazy notion that you—"

Footsteps coming into the store from the back room cut Ashley off mid-sentence.

"Hey Ash, you'll never guess what happened in the alley." Chad rushed up to her but stopped just short of Heather. "I didn't know *you* were here. Thought you'd be having a leisurely lunch with *someone*."

She wished she'd said something at the time, but hopefully now he would listen. "Honestly, Chad. I was just making a joke earlier. I never thought you'd take me seriously. Who could I possibly ask to lunch besides my aunt?"

"I thought maybe you'd ask your ex since he's in town now."

"You know I loathe Jack for the way he treated me in the past. I would never ask him anything, much less invite him to lunch."

Chad's shoulders relaxed. He stared into her eyes, and a small smile crossed his lips.

Julia made an appearance from behind a tall bookshelf. "I'm here too."

"Of course you are," Chad deadpanned.

This wouldn't have been a surprise. She'd been in the bookstore every day this week, looking through their occult books, trying to find the perfect anti-curse ritual.

"Did Krystal really find a man lying by our back door when she was jogging?" Ashley asked in an excited voice.

"Yeah. I just spoke with her. She must have been really shaken up, because she hung her arms around my neck until the police pried her off and took her to the station to make a statement. She said she found him around noon."

"Krystal was jogging here at noon?" Heather asked. "That seems like an unusual time to jog. Most people do it early in the morning or after sunset, especially in his heat."

"Not unusual for Krystal," Ashley said. "She lives by her own set of rules."

I'm not even going there. No doubt she was spying on Chad, especially since she probably views me as competition, and she knows I live upstairs.

"Any idea who he is?" Heather asked.

"I don't. All I saw was a man's body lying at the foot of the stairs, head twisted to one side, eyes wide open, as if he'd seen something horrible."

Julia gasped and turned to face a bookcase. She leaned into Heather and whispered, "What did I tell you about seeing death in the cards?"

This seemed too coincidental. "Is there something you want to get off your chest?" she asked her aunt.

Julia pointed to the occult book in her hand. "Remember, I told you demons and gargoyles were watching and waiting for some kind of signal from Beelzebub to do evil? Maybe the signal is what this man saw, and that's why his face looked the way it did."

"I doubt it," Heather said. "I'm sure he was just scared by whatever or *whoever* it is that killed him."

Chad glanced at her and then at Julia. Her aunt's words didn't seem to phase him, probably because Julia had been talking about occult things for the past couple of weeks. Heather could only imagine what he must be thinking.

"Anyway," Chad started again, "the coroner came and took him. Looks like he might have had some kind of accident or a heart attack. That's all the information I have right now."

"Could he be someone who lives in town?" Ashley asked.

"I didn't recognize him, and I couldn't get his name. He looked middle-aged to me. Early fifties maybe. Salt and pepper hair, day old beard. He had on a white short-sleeved shirt and khaki pants."

Chad picked up the books Julia had just returned. "Oh yeah, there was one thing I noticed that seemed kind of odd for a man in this town. He was wearing Gucci loafers."

Julia's shoulders rose and fell as if she'd taken a deep breath and let it out. She put a hand over her heart.

"Do you know him?" Heather asked.

Julia's eyes widened. "Who me? How would I know him?" She casually flipped though the pages of the book in her hand with her brows raised. "Define know."

Uh oh, this doesn't sound good.

"Aunt Julia?" Heather's voice rose to a higher pitch. "What do you know about this man?"

With all eyes on her, Julia shrank back and set the book on the shelf. She didn't meet Heather's gaze. "Nothing, really. I heard someone walking on the back stairs this morning. It sounded like he stopped at our door. And then I heard some thumping noises and went to get my baseball bat in case he might be a burglar. If he'd have broken in, he would have gotten the surprise of his life."

Trying to keep a positive attitude about the situation, Heather said, "Maybe he was looking for your grandfather." She'd had this experience once before. "He wouldn't be the first man who didn't know your granddad had passed away and came to his apartment looking for him."

Chad shrugged. "He could have been one of my grandfather's cronies. Granddad knew a lot of people from all walks of life."

A moment later, the front door burst open with a tinkle, and dozens of residents crowded into the small book shop, all talking at once. Heather moved to a less occupied aisle and found her aunt.

Curious people asked Chad and Ashley about what happened in the alley. Evidently, they'd seen it on the newsfeed that went live on the scene, and they wanted to know who the man was and what he was doing in their alley on a Sunday morning when the store wasn't open yet.

A loud meow came from somewhere above their heads. Heather looked up. Makki paced along the top of the highest bookshelf as if searching for a place to jump down into the middle of the crowd.

She didn't want to be around to witness that, so she grabbed Julia's arm and guided her to the back room and out the door where dozens more residents had gathered to check out the scene, along with a couple of news people with cameras and microphones.

They had to squeeze past several police officers who'd been stationed there, to get out of the store. Someone recognized them as the ladies who lived upstairs, and the questions started from the reporters as microphones were shoved in their faces. "Who was the man? Did they know him? Did he have an accident? What happened to him? Why was he in the alley? Was he new in town? Did you see or hear anything?"

Heather didn't know the answers to any of their questions, but she didn't know if her aunt did. If she had to be on camera this morning, at least she was dressed for it.

Julia stood with her arms folded across her chest, her rose red lips pressed tight, ignoring the microphone in her face.

Heather turned toward the crowd and pushed a few stray strands of hair from her face. She waved her arms, trying to draw their attention.

"Listen, everyone. We don't know anything. We're as curious about what happened as you. So, we're sorry. We can't help, because we don't have any answers."

The crowd gave out a collective sound of disappointment as the news people took the microphones down and cut the cameras. Heather guided her aunt to the side entrance to their apartment where no one was standing.

She made it half way up the stairs and spotted Jack standing on the top landing. He must have been waiting for her to get home. Just what she didn't need right now.

Chapter 4

HEATHER tried to push past Jack. "What are you doing here? I told you I'd call when I was free."

"I said I needed to talk to you, and now look what's happened. Why don't you ever listen to me? This is important!"

Julia unlocked the door and strolled in. Heather followed her. Jack sauntered in behind them, taking in the room. "Wow. Vintage seventies. Love the bookshelf wall."

He strolled around and made his way past the gold, brocade sofa and toward the back of the room where the large fireplace was the focal point. "They don't make fireplaces like this anymore." He tapped the pine mantle. "Solid but too old-fashioned for me. Time to redecorate."

Heather couldn't let his comments go. Why did he always put her on the defensive? "The apartment came furnished."

Julia ambled into the galley kitchen. "Can I get either of you something to drink?"

"No, we don't want anything to drink. And he's not staying." Heather whirled on Jack. "What did you mean when you said, 'Look what's happened now?'"

He glanced in Julia's direction. "I'd love something to drink, thanks."

Jack made himself comfortable on the sofa and crossed his legs. A moment later, Makki jumped on the top of the sofa and stared down at him. He raised his hackles and hissed.

"Ugh, a cat! You know I hate cats." Jack shoved him off.

The cat dropped to the floor with a thump and a yowl.

"Hey! Stop that!" Heather stooped down, picked up the cat, and cradled him in her arms. "It's okay, Makki. I've got you now. The big bully won't hurt you again."

She ran a tender hand over his sleek back as he purred.

Jack scrunched his nose. "Is he yours?"

"No, he lives downstairs, so he's around a lot. If you have a problem with that, you can leave."

Jack grimaced. "I can live with it. Just keep him away from me. Now where's that drink I was promised?"

She sighed in defeat. "What do you want?"

"You know what I like, Heather."

Hot blood rushed to her face as she set the cat on the floor. The man was insufferable. He still expected her to wait on him. *How did I put up with it for so long?* But if a drink would get the sandy-haired egomaniac out the door any sooner, she was glad to make that odd concoction he enjoyed so much.

Heather put three ice cubes in a tall glass and then filled it to the top with equal parts Pepsi and ginger ale. She stomped up to him and shoved the glass into his hand.

He chugged the entire contents, sans the ice cubes. After a few moments, and a long belch, he clinked the cubes around and called out, "Refill."

Did he think she was going to accommodate him, again? She hated his stalling tactics, and how he loved to use them when he wanted to drag out a situation. Evidently, he wasn't in any hurry to get back to Chicago.

She stood her ground, hands on her hips. "No refills. Just tell me."

Jack hesitated a moment, as if he was thinking things over. "Okay, but you're not going to like it."

Aunt Julia came out of the kitchen with a soft drink in her hand. "I'll leave you two alone to talk."

Jack pushed himself off the sofa. "No. Wait, Julia. What I have to say concerns you too."

She stopped, her brows raised. "Oh?"

Jack's gaze turned to Heather. "Did you know your aunt owes a huge favor to an unscrupulous, big-time crook? She knows who I mean."

Jack and Julia stared at each other as if they shared an appalling secret.

Heather had no idea what was going on between them. "Is this true?" she asked her aunt.

Julia stood with her hands on her hips. "If I do, what's it got to do with you, Jack?"

"The man himself came to my office two weeks ago looking for you. He'd found out I was dating your niece and wanted her address so she could tell him where you live."

"And so you gave it to him?" Heather huffed. *How thoughtless.*

Jack turned to her. "I just gave him the name of the town. I was angry with you for ignoring me. Then I started feeling guilty and thought I should warn you about him, in case this guy came to your door looking for your aunt. But you wouldn't read my emails or take my calls, so I had to come here in person to clue you in, but I didn't know she was living with you."

Heather was surprised he had the decency to travel all that way. "Thanks for coming here to tell us. So, who is this guy?"

Julia paced the living room floor, wringing her fingers, her eyes scrunched in a painful look. "It's Jimmy the Horse."

"Why does he want to contact you?" Then a scary thought struck Heather, and she gasped. "What kind of favor do you owe him?"

Julia waved her question away. "Nothing... really. I just walked away from a situation I didn't want to deal with, like I always do. And that should have been the end of it."

Heather's stomach dropped. "What kind of situation? Is this guy dangerous? Does he want to kill you?"

Julia shook her head. "Noooo. At least, I don't think he does."

"How can you be so sure?"

"Because he loves me."

Heather dropped her tense shoulders. "Huh? I don't understand."

"The man is smitten. He wants me to marry him, but after years of making the same mistakes with men over and over, now I know better. Besides, I don't trust him. He's got those snaky-looking eyes that frighten me."

Heather couldn't imagine Julia being afraid of any man. She turned back to Jack, exasperated. "What in the world is she talking about?"

He shrugged. "I don't know, but I can't wait to hear what your aunt has to say."

Julia finished the soft drink in her glass. "It's like this. I'd been working as a magician's assistant. That's when I was much younger and more attractive. The guy I worked for was a fabulous close up card magician. He taught me a lot about cards. How to count them without anyone noticing and how to manipulate them so no one would catch on. Plus, he was the hottest guy who had come along in my life in years. We were so much in love. I mean, we couldn't keep our hands off each other. But as it turned out, he was the devil is disguise."

Heather could just imagine. As a young woman, Julia was daring, charming, and absolutely lovely. Everyone adored her. She'd had every advantage too—wealth, education, looks. But she also had a bad habit of falling in love with the wrong men.

"Go on." Heather said in an encouraging voice.

"One day, he asked me if I would be interested in making a lot of money in one afternoon. I was always desperate for money back then. The job of small-time magician's assistant didn't pay much. He wanted me to work as his shill in a high-stakes poker game."

"And before you ask, Heather," Jack said. "High-stakes poker is illegal in Illinois. But you knew that, didn't you, Julia?"

"Of course I knew that, but I was in Vegas at the time. I was head over heels in love, and I had no idea this guy was just using me. Besides, I enjoyed playing poker, and I was excellent at manipulating cards. I thought as long as this job was for one night only, what harm could it do?"

"That's quite a story," Heather said. "So how does Jimmy the Horse fit into this scenario?"

"After playing cards that afternoon, I found out the magician was married, and if that wasn't bad enough, he refused to split the winnings. I was so angry, I grabbed what money I could get my hands on and scrambled straight to the nearest race track. But because I was so upset, I was losing badly that day."

Julia rubbed her eyes. "Jimmy, who always hung around the track, or so I'd heard, happened to notice, and took me under his wing. He knew a lot of the jockeys, the trainers, and some of the owners. He taught me most of what I know about betting on horses. Guess you might say he was my rebound guy from the unscrupulous magician. Too bad he didn't know me better, because as it turned out, he was the one who got conned. Not a good idea now that I look back on it."

Heather dragged her hands over her face. "It doesn't sound like there's a happy ending to this story."

"It depends on who's ending you're talking about." Julia sighed. "One day, I got caught in the middle of one of Jimmy's cons by an undercover FBI agent. Only I didn't know Jimmy was conning someone until they explained to me how he was doing it. I told you I was in federal prison for a while. Well, overnight anyway. The next morning, I made a deal with them and turned Jimmy in. I felt bad, but it was his own fault for using me that way. He'd been so good to me until then, I didn't know what to say. So I told Jimmy that when he got out of prison, I owed him big time. You know, the way you do, but you don't really mean it. I didn't think I'd ever see him again."

Heather's mind raced. "You did the right thing by turning him in to the Feds."

Julia held up a hand. "I did it to save my own neck."

"Do you think the guy on our back steps was sent by Jimmy to find you?"

"Maybe." Julia rubbed her arms as if she'd suddenly gotten a chill. "Or he might be a thief who has nothing to do with any of this."

Chapter 5

JULIA wasn't often this wishy-washy about a subject. Her opinions were pretty straight forward.

Heather stared at her aunt. "Too bad we won't find out who the man is until his identification is released by the police."

Jack's cell phone vibrated. He glanced at it. "Now that you know everything, I'm going."

"Back to Chicago, I hope." The words poured out before Heather could stop them. *That sounded a little cruel, but knowing Jack, it probably went right over his head.*

Jack sauntered to the door with a snicker on his lips. "No. Right now, I'm going back to the off-track betting place. Thanks for telling me about it. The proprietor, Krystal Stamos, is smokin' hot. But that accountant of hers, Johnny Tanner, has got to go. He thinks he owns her."

Heather hoped Krystal and Jack got together. Two narcissistic hearts beating as one. *I think I'll give him a little more incentive to try and get her away from Tanner.*

"Just for your information, Krystal was also an underwear model in New York until a few weeks ago." *That news will probably make him sprint there.*

Whatever was going on behind those shifty gray eyes, Jack wasn't sharing, but he wiped imaginary sweat from his brow. "I'll find a way to get past this Tanner guy." He let himself out and closed the door behind him.

Heather watched the street from the living room window. As he crossed it, he nodded to a tall, thin man.

Julia glanced out. "What are you looking at?"

"I just wanted to make sure Jack was actually leaving and not waiting for me downstairs. He's across the street now, and he just gestured to that tall man standing on the corner."

Julia gasped and turned away from the window as the man headed toward the bookstore.

"What's wrong? Do you know him?"

Julia's face turned a dull shade of putty. "It's Jimmy the Horse."

Heather shook with anger. "Jack's done some pretty despicable things in his life, but leading Jimmy right to your door is too much."

"It's all right." Julia popped a tiny mint into her mouth and calmed down in the blink of an eye. She smoothed her hair. "How do I look?" Without waiting for an answer, she ran to her bedroom.

Heather followed.

Julia assessed her face in the mirror over her dresser. Then she grabbed her brush and attempted to tame her wild, shoulder-length, fire-engine red hair. Afterward, she glazed her lips with bright red lipstick and tapped rose rouge on her cheeks.

She turned toward Heather. "Does this outfit look okay?"

The red and pink flowered blouse over her fitted red capri slacks were a little tight, and on the loud side, but then so was everything in her aunt's wardrobe.

"Yes, it's definitely you," Heather said. "But I don't understand. Don't you want to run out the back door? I thought you were afraid of this guy."

"I refuse to let *him* know that."

Heather was at a loss for words as her heart beat against her chest. She reached into her jeans pocket and handed her aunt the pepper spray container.

Julia pushed it away. "That's not necessary. I can handle this guy. He's just an ex-con. I've gone up against worse." She tapped her chin with three fingers. "Of course, I was a lot younger then."

Small comfort.

Julia pushed Heather toward the back door. "Go. I don't want him to see you here."

There was no way Heather was leaving her aunt in the apartment alone with that crook. She slipped out the back door as a knock came on the front. But instead of closing it behind her, Heather left it open a crack so she could peek inside and hear what they were saying… and maybe call for help if her aunt got into trouble.

Chapter 6

JULIA opened the door, but Heather couldn't see anyone.

A baritone voice said, "Well, if it isn't Julie Summers. Aren't you a sight for sore eyes?"

"Summers?" Heather whispered. *He must have known her before she was married.*

"Jimmy the Horse." Julia took a few steps back to let him in. "I wish I could say the same."

"Don't be like that, sweetheart." He strolled around the living room.

Heather caught a glimpse of the man. Tall, maybe six-three, and thin as a rail. He had a leathery-looking face with a dark tan, or maybe that was just the color of his skin. She'd expected him to be a hefty man with a nickname like "The Horse." But it looked like her aunt could knock this guy over with one good push.

A slight whooshing sound came from the living room as if he'd plopped down on the sofa.

Julia tsked. "Make yourself at home." Sarcasm dripped from every word.

"I always do."

"Now that you've found me, what do you want?"

"It's been over twenty years, and I've spent a lot of money and resources trying to track you down. You know what I want."

"Two fingers of Crown Royal?"

"I wouldn't mind, if it'll start a conversation."

Julia sauntered to the kitchen, where Heather could get a better view of what she was doing. Her aunt placed both hands on the counter and leaned forward. She stood there a couple of moments, as if she was trying to pull her thoughts together. Then she took a deep breath and let it out in one big whoosh. She grabbed a couple of juice glasses, along with the whiskey bottle from the top cabinet, and poured out a measure of whiskey in each. Then she put one glass to her lips and tossed back the contents.

Jimmy came up behind her and put his arms around her waist. She turned, pushed him away, and shoved the other glass into his right hand. He tossed back his whiskey and slammed the glass down on the counter. "I guess that's a start."

"You want another?"

"No, Julia. I want you."

Heather sucked in a breath. She covered her mouth in case an errant noise escaped.

Julia folded her arms at her waist. "Well, you can't have me!"

His dark eyes sharpened to anger. "Boy Julia, you're a pistol!" The muscles tightened around his mouth. "First you hand me over to the Feds, then you take off to God knows where with my stuff. You said you owed me big time when I got out, and I'm here to collect what's mine."

Julia held up a finger. "Correction. It's *mine*, and I have every right to it."

He shook his head. "Don't try and con *me*. I want it, now."

"Stop saying that!" Julia tapped the counter with her long, red nails in an anxious gesture. "How did you find out where I live?"

"When I sent Denny Serrano to find your niece and track you down, he never expected you to be living in Willows Bend, too. Until he saw you here. I'm surprised you didn't recognize him. He's been hanging around this town for over a week."

Julia scrunched her eyes. "I wasn't looking for him. Why would I think he was here?"

"He looked a little different, but not so much that you wouldn't have known him. He got his nose broke and reset."

"The perks of being your strong-arm guy?"

"Never mind the wise-cracks. What about you? Denny almost didn't recognize you. Let's face it, you put on more than a few pounds since I saw you last." He eyed her from head to toe. "And what's with the crazy, loud clothes? And that hideous, bright red hair? It almost looks like you're in hiding."

Heather thought a moment. *Come to think of it, I nearly didn't recognize her either when I ran into her a few weeks ago at the train station.*

Julia pulled herself up to her full five-feet-eight-inches, sucked in a deep breath, and placed her hands on her waist. "Did you come all this way to insult me?"

"No, baby. I came here to get you back. Got any ideas what happened to Denny?"

Julia shook her head. "The first I knew about him, the guy was down at the bottom of my stairs, probably dead."

He gazed at her through narrowed eyes. "Are you sure? Maybe you gave him one of your infamous shoves."

Heather pulled her head away from the door. She had a feeling her aunt had been hiding something. *Infamous shoves? I'll have to ask.*

At least Julia could now tell the police she knew the guy who'd been stalking her. But would she? Heather couldn't imagine why not, but then, she never knew what her aunt would or wouldn't do.

Heather rubbed her bottom lip with her thumbnail, a nervous habit from her childhood, and put her ear to the door to hear more of their conversation.

"So give it over." Jimmy said.

"What are you talking about?" Julia sounded surprised. "Give *what* over?"

"You absconded with it, and I want it back."

"If you're talking about the money," Julia said, "I lost it playing the horses years ago."

"That's not what I'm talking about, and you know it."

Footsteps on the stairs startled Heather.

"What are you doing out here?" Chad's voice drowned out the conversation happening inside.

She put a finger to her lips. "Shhh. I can't hear."

A moment later, the back door swung open.

In a panic, Heather flung her arms around Chad's neck and kissed him. His soft, warm lips responded. He put his arms around her, pulled her tight against him, and deepened the kiss. Her heart raced like a school girl's on her first date.

It felt so right, she could have stayed like that all day if it weren't for a loud, baritone voice saying, "Make love where you pay the rent."

The back door slammed shut.

At the sound, Heather flinched and broke the kiss. She took her arms from around Chad's neck, and he released her.

She shook her head to clear the fog. "I didn't know what else to do. I'm sorry."

"I'm not." Chad gave her an understanding smile that warmed her all over. "I've wanted to do that from the moment we met."

Unable to focus on anything but that breathtaking kiss, Heather gazed into his eyes. "Then why didn't you?"

He jerked his head back and squinted as if he couldn't believe she asked that. "And get my face slapped? You didn't know me then." A moment of uncomfortable silence passed between them before he asked, "You still haven't answered my question. What were you doing out here when I showed up?"

"I'll explain, but we can't talk here."

Chapter 7

CHAD opened the back door of the bookstore. "Since there are customers in the front, we can stay in here and talk."

Heather glanced at the ceiling, and her eyes grazed the air return vent where, from her bedroom upstairs, she could hear every word being said in this room, and Makki managed to squeeze through to get into her apartment. She couldn't chance her aunt hearing them or telling Chad she'd been eavesdropping. Besides, she loved having the cat upstairs and wasn't averse to overhearing an occasional conversation between brother and sister, if it concerned her.

Before Chad shut the door behind them, Heather said, "Can we go someplace else?"

He shook his head. "Sorry, I can't leave the store right now—too many customers for my sister to handle alone. I was just going to check if the alley was clear of TV reporters when I saw you on the second-floor landing."

She wasn't surprised he spotted her. The back stairs were made of wood with a slim railing leading up to a short landing on the second floor, where she and her aunt lived, and then up another flight of stairs to the attic landing. All out in the open where anyone passing by could see.

"Let me just make a call." She patted her sides where her pockets should be, but the thin sun dress she wore didn't have any. "I don't have my phone. I have to go back upstairs right now. Can we talk later?"

He shortened the space between them and gazed into her eyes. "Have dinner with me tonight. We can talk then."

I thought he'd never ask. "But don't you usually eat with your sister?"

"Not lately. She's been having dinner and spending every evening with Miklos Vendeglo at his Hungarian restaurant."

"I didn't know she was still dating him."

"Yes, and for the life of me I can't understand why. He's such a..."

"Handsome guy?" Heather finished.

She wasn't just saying that. Unlike Sandos, his short, unattractive, muscle-bound brother, Miklos really was handsome with his black curly hair, dark smoldering eyes, and features that made it appear as if he might be descended from pirate stock. Not to mention that sexy swagger. Most of the young females in Willows Bend had a crush on him, but he seemed to only have eyes for Ashley, the prettiest girl in town.

"That's not what I was going to say." Chad smiled. "But let's not get into it now. Why don't I pick you up at seven-thirty. I'll take you to a little secluded place I know where we can talk in private."

As much as she wanted to go, the uncertainty of her aunt being home alone with that crook held her back. "There's nothing I would enjoy more, but I don't know if I can leave my aunt tonight. I'll let you know."

Chad's cell phone pinged. "My sister's looking for me. Hopefully I'll see you later."

Heather left the store wrapped in a blanket of happiness. She and Chad had their first kiss, and he finally asked her to dinner. She'd almost forgotten her worries about her aunt as she tiptoed up the stairs. At the landing, she turned the door knob and pushed the back door open a crack.

Her aunt glanced at the door. "It's okay, Heather, you can come in now. He's gone."

Aunt Julia sat at the kitchen counter on the edge of a stool, shuffling a deck of playing cards. "Why did you hang around on the back landing when I told you to leave? What happened to our privacy pact—as in, 'you give me some, and I'll give you some'?"

Heather put on her most sincere frown. "I'm sorry. I know it was an invasion of your privacy, but I was worried about you being alone with that felon, and I thought you might need help at some point."

Julia rubbed a hand over her forehead as if she was trying to decide what to say. "I assured you that I could take care of whatever situation came up."

"I should have believed you. You've proven yourself more than once. All I can say is, I'm sorry. It won't happen again."

"Well, it better not." Julia gave her a wide smile. "It's just that I'm so used to taking care of myself, it feels awkward when someone else wants to take care of me."

Heather put an arm around her aunt's thick shoulder. "I'll always take care of you."

Julia patted Heather's hand. "I know you will." She shuffled the cards and laid a few down on the Formica countertop, face up.

"Are you going to play Solitaire?"

"No. I'm seeing what my future holds."

"Why use playing cards and not a Tarot deck?"

"I don't mess with Tarot. Too much like the occult, and I've had enough of that lately. This is known as Cartomancy. That cheating magician taught me a lot more about cards than just how to win at poker."

"And you really believe in this sort of thing?"

"Of course." Julia patted the chair next to her, and Heather sat.

Why am I surprised? If she believes in curses, of course she believes in magical fortune telling playing cards.

Julia scooped up the cards and shuffled the deck again. "Cartomancy can be traced back to Europe as far as the thirteen hundreds, or somewhere around there. It was the favorite pastime of the royals in European courts."

"I didn't know that."

"What *do* you know about a playing card deck?"

"Just the basics. Fifty-two cards, four suits, Ace is the high card."

"There's more meaning to the cards than just the obvious. For instance, the fifty-two cards represent the fifty-two weeks in a year, and the four suits represent the four seasons. Thirteen cards in a suit equal the thirteen weeks in each season. Twelve royals represent the twelve months."

Heather put a hand to her forehead in a gesture of frustration. "This is all very interesting, but you can explain it to me another time. Right now, I have more important things on my mind."

Julia set the deck on the counter. "More important than seeing what the future holds?"

"Right now, yes," Heather said. "Like your conversation with Jimmy the Horse, for one."

Julia sighed and pursed her red lips as if she was almost ashamed of what they had said. "How much did you hear?"

"Everything up until Jimmy opened the back door."

Julia snickered. "When he heard people talking on the landing, he got furious and demanded to know what was going on out there."

"What did you say?"

"I told him it was probably the people who live upstairs."

Heather couldn't help but laugh. "In the attic? The only things living up there are some spiders and the occasional bat."

Julia waved her hand. "He doesn't know that."

"It does explain why he said we should make love where we pay the rent."

"That's funny." Julia said. "Who were you talking to out there, anyway?"

Heather filled a glass with bottled water and took a sip. All this talking was making her throat dry. "It was so embarrassing. Chad came up the stairs and asked me why I was there. Then, the back door opened, and I panicked. I threw my arms around Chad's neck and kissed him."

"Clever," Julia said. "It's about time you two got together. But I don't want you, or him, to be involved in my affairs if it can be helped. Especially now that you're going to work for the mayor."

Heather gulped more water. "I forgot about that. But it's too late. We're already involved."

Chapter 8

"GREAT." Julia poured two fingers of Crown Royal in a juice glass and swallowed it down in one gulp. "Jack knows all about this now. But how much does Chad know?"

"He knows a lot of it." *And I'm going to tell him the rest if we go to dinner tonight.*

Julia shook her head as if she was disgusted with the whole situation.

Heather shrugged. "I had to explain why I kissed him so suddenly."

"It's okay." Julia paced the floor. "Especially since you two will probably start dating now."

Heather rubbed her thumbnail across her bottom lip. "I don't know about all that. It was just one kiss." She sighed as she thought of the way his lips were so responsive. "But we are having dinner."

"Did he ask you, or did you ask him?"

"He asked me."

Julia put a hand out for emphasis. "I rest my case."

"The reason he invited me was because he usually eats with his sister, but she's having dinner with Miklos Vendeglo at his restaurant tonight. Chad probably doesn't like to eat alone."

Julia wagged a finger at Heather. "Why didn't you invite him up here for dinner with us?"

"I didn't know what was going on with you and Jimmy. And besides... I didn't think of it."

"I know. You want to be alone with him, and I don't blame you. He's an attractive man."

Heather smiled. Her aunt was extremely perceptive. "You're right. But sorry, Aunt Julia, now you'll have to eat dinner alone."

"I'm not eating alone. I'm having dinner with Jimmy. We have a few things we need to straighten out."

"You mean, like what he wants from you?"

Julia's red lips flattened. "You heard that, huh?"

"Yes and a lot more. What did he want you to give back to him?"

"Oh..." She gave Heather a wary side glance that said there was more to this story than she wanted to admit. "Probably what I walked away with."

"Which was?"

"About two hundred thou, give or take."

Heather sucked in a breath. "Dollars?"

"Of course dollars. It certainly wasn't butterscotch candies."

"Where did you get all that money?"

"Betting on horses and playing the casino tables and slots, things like that. You can't play unless you have the money to back up your bets. And I was riding high in those days. Until I got arrested by the Feds."

"Was it Jimmy's money you were playing with?"

"Some of it was at first, but I worked real hard to make my own money off the initial stake he lent me, so what I won was mine."

"What happened to it all, if you don't mind my asking?"

Julia shrugged. "I invested in a broken-down race horse. Jimmy wasn't the only con man around. I bought a diamond bracelet and a ring to match, to go with my fancy sports car. Come to think of it, the car was a bad investment. I should have stuck to jewelry. Unfortunately, I hung out with the worst bunch of swindlers you'd ever want to meet. The money was gone within six months, and so were the diamonds. Much faster than you could ever imagine."

Heather leaned against the back of her stool for support. *How could someone lose all that money so quickly?* "I guess it's true what they say... Easy come, easy go."

Julia huffed. "I earned every penny of it, and I don't care what Jimmy says. That money was mine! I owe him nothing."

"But it sounds like he thinks you do."

"What he says, and what we both know to be true, are two different things. I'm tired of his nasty insinuations and false accusations, so once and for all, we're going to have it out." Her dark eyes flashed as she raised a finger. "Tonight!"

Aunt Julia sounded adamant, which really worried Heather. But then, she promised to give her aunt some privacy... and she would... this time at least. So while she had her qualms about going out tonight, she'd have to put them aside and trust Julia. Besides, she really wanted to go to dinner with Chad.

She sent him a text, accepting his invitation.

Just as an added precaution, Heather checked to see if Detective Lindsey was on duty at the police station this evening. Luckily, he was. It put her mind at ease, knowing he was around in case of trouble. And with her aunt out with Jimmy the Horse, there might very well be.

<><><>

With a lighter heart, Heather rummaged through her closet for something to wear. She couldn't wear the same dress to dinner that she'd worn for lunch. She found a v-neck, pale turquoise, above-the-knee, wrap dress that hugged her curves and showed a little cleavage.

She put a few hot rollers in her hair and freshened up her makeup for the evening. By the time she'd combed out and arranged her hair, Julia was gone. Heather made up her mind not to worry. It wouldn't help the situation and would only make her stomach so tight, she wouldn't be able to enjoy her dinner or her time with Chad.

As she waited for him to arrive, she emailed her resume to the mayor and kept her fingers crossed that the incident at the back stairs didn't kill her chances of getting the job.

At seven-thirty, the doorbell rang. She gave herself a quick check, grabbed her white clutch bag, and answered it. Chad stood near the threshold wearing a short sleeved, pale green shirt and chinos.

He took a step back as he gazed at her. "You look lovely."

"Thanks." Heather stepped out and locked the door. "Are we going to a restaurant in town?"

Chad followed her down the stairs. "Yes and no."

Chapter 9

CHAD's black Lexus LX made its way down Main Street past all the boutiques, the movie theater, the ice cream parlor, and The Athena restaurant.

Heather couldn't imagine where they were going. "We're either staying in town or we're not. Which is it?"

"Actually, it's both."

They drove another few miles toward the edge of town, and just as Heather was enjoying the gold and mauve of the sun setting behind the tall trees, Chad made a sharp right turn into a cemetery. Eerie shades of gray and dark shadows crept over the ancient crumbling tombstones. The dilapidated mausoleums looked to be about a hundred years old.

"Why are we driving through here? It looks like the cemetery my aunt and I were lost in a couple of weeks ago."

"It is." He switched on his headlights. "When I was looking for you, I found an old building I'd forgotten about."

"We're not eating in the cemetery, are we? I mean, I know it's private and secluded, but it's not exactly what I had in mind as a dinner venue."

"Of course not. This is a shortcut. A smile creased his lips. "Trust me."

Those two words from a man were never a good sign. She was beginning to regret accepting his dinner invitation.

After driving on a seemingly endless, winding road, they finally passed out of the cemetery through the tall, rusted iron gate on the other side. Chad turned onto the highway for a mile or two before he pulled in behind a one-story brick building with a dozen cars parked in its gravel driveway. The only window in the building was a small glass block in the middle where a fluorescent light shone with a red square logo and the name of a craft beer she didn't recognize.

They got out of the car, and Chad took her hand. He led her to a solid metal door painted a dark red.

She looked up at him. "Where are we?"

"The Blue Moon Hideaway."

Her eyes widened, and she couldn't help the smile that spread across her lips. "Sounds wicked."

He opened the door for her, and she stepped into a small vestibule with a dark wooden door in front of her. Chad knocked four times. A small, square peephole opened in the door, and he whispered something to whoever was standing behind it. The peephole closed, and the larger door opened to admit them.

In the dim interior of the room, murmurs could barely be heard, and shadowy images of faces passed as a short man wearing a white shirt, black vest, and black pants led them to a small table in a corner where he lit a candle in a round, stained glass holder. Then he handed each a silver plated drink menu.

After they were seated, the man asked, "What can I get you to drink?"

Chad bent over the table and in a low voice asked, "What would you like?"

Heather opened the silver menu and studied the list of drinks she could barely make out in the candlelight. At the top of the list were two vintages of Champagne. She loved Champagne. The first on the list was a Duval-Leroy Brut Reserve she found to be too expensive. But the second, Tattinger Brut La Francaise, cost quite a bit less, not to mention she adored the taste.

"I'll have a small bottle of the Tattinger Champagne."

Chad glanced up and handed the man their drink menus. "I'll have the same."

"You're a champagne drinker?" Heather asked as the man disappeared into the darkness.

Chad nodded. "You seem surprised."

"I took you for a scotch rocks kind of guy, being a former P.I."

"It depends on who I'm with and what I'm doing."

"I love to drink champagne anytime. And since I wasn't sure what I was going to eat..." Heather shrugged. "In my opinion, Champagne goes with everything."

"Good point." A half smile creased his lips. "I'll be sure to keep some Tattinger well-stocked for you. Any special vintage?"

She shook her head. "I'm sorry if I gave you the impression I drink it all the time. I don't. I couldn't afford it for one thing, and I'm not much of a drinker for another."

He leaned back in his seat and crossed his arms. "I'm glad you straightened that out."

Just as he said the words, a man came to the table with two small bottles of champagne and two flutes. "Would you like to see a menu?"

Heather nodded.

But Chad asked, "What's your special tonight?"

"Shrimp cocktails and Chateaubriand for two with Chateau potatoes and spring vegetables."

Heather couldn't stop smiling. She was so hungry. She hadn't eaten anything since that small crab salad at lunch. "Sounds delicious."

"We'll have the Special," Chad said.

"Very good." The man turned and walked away.

Chad poured a flute of Champagne for Heather from her bottle and one for himself from his.

Heather lifted her glass. "What shall we drink to?"

"How about... to new beginnings."

Heather clinked glasses with him. "New beginnings." She took a sip. She hadn't felt this happy and comfortable with a man in a long time. *I wish this moment could last forever.*

He gazed at her through his glass. "You look beautiful tonight. I love your hair that way."

She thought her heart would burst. "Thank you."

He didn't even have to try. She was already falling in love with him. Too bad he wasn't aware of it. She wanted to tell him, but the little voice at the back of her mind reminded her it was too early to say the "L" word. After all, she'd just broken up with Jack, and she didn't want Chad to be her rebound guy. Theirs was a relationship she wanted to last for a long time. So she changed the subject.

"It's quiet in here, even though there seemed to be a lot of customers when we walked in."

He pointed to the dark walls and black ceiling. "Acoustic tiles. It quiets the noise so we can talk in private."

"How did you find this place?"

"It's been here for as long as I can remember, but it's changed hands many times over the years. I just rediscovered it when I was searching for you and your aunt around the old cemetery a couple of weeks ago. The new manager told me it had been a speakeasy in the thirties, thus the two front doors and two back doors. One set of doors is in town and the other out of town."

Heather scrunched her eyes. "I don't understand. How did the building get that way?"

"It was originally built as a roadhouse, but the boundaries of the town weren't clear cut at that time, so the builder put the building up on the land that was owned by his client, which turned out to be in the middle of the demarcation line between the town and the forest preserve. So the east side of the building is in town, and the west side is outside town limits."

She smiled. "How unusual."

Out of the darkness, the waiter wheeled over a couple of shrimp cocktails on a small cart and set them on the table along with several slices of warm bread in a basket and a few pats of butter on a silver plate.

Once the waiter left, Heather dug into the cocktail. It was delicious, but there wasn't much of it. She could have eaten two.

Chad finished his shrimp before she did and was now munching a slice of bread and butter. "So, are you going to tell me why you kissed me on your back porch this afternoon?"

Chapter 10

HEATHER nearly choked on the sip of champagne she'd just taken. It wasn't as if she hadn't been expecting the question. After all, that was why they went out to dinner, to talk in private.

Chad put his bread down and gazed at her across the table. "I believe it has something to do with your aunt."

Heather took another sip of wine to clear her throat. "Yes, it does. I was trying to stop you from talking."

The sparkle in Chad's eyes fizzled out, as if she'd flipped a switch. "So you would have kissed any man who came along?"

"No, of course not. I probably would have just put my hand over his mouth and told him to be quiet."

"Then why didn't you do that to me?"

"I panicked. I was trying to hide the fact that I was standing outside the back door listening to her conversation because I thought she might need help."

Chad grinned. "It's funny. I never took you for an eavesdropper."

"My aunt is an exception."

"I can understand how you feel after everything that's happened to her in the past few weeks, but you've already told me the part about listening at the door. Why did you think she might need help?"

As the entree was served and eaten, Heather explained about her aunt's association with the magician, the high-stakes poker game, Jimmy the Horse, his con games at the track, the money he thought she owed him, his marriage proposal, and the guy at the bottom of the stairs, who she identified as Jimmy's strong-arm man, Denny Serrano.

Chad wiped his lips with his napkin and set it down next to his empty plate. "That's quite a story. Are you sure your aunt wanted you to tell me all this?"

"I told her I should keep you informed. Since you knew some of it, you should know all of it. As things stand, I think she might need your help at some point." Heather set her fork and knife on her plate.

"I can't imagine what I could possibly do to help her. You forget, I'm not a P.I. anymore. But she *might* need a good lawyer."

The waiter appeared at the table and asked if either of them wanted dessert.

Chad looked to her for an answer.

"No thank you," she said. "I couldn't eat another bite."

"Coffee?"

Heather checked her cell phone. *Ten-thirty*. They'd been talking for hours, and yet it felt as if only a few minutes had passed. "I'm not in the mood for coffee. I didn't realize it was so late. I've got a job to get to tomorrow morning."

Chad waved the waiter away. "No coffee for me either. Thanks." He finished the few drops of champagne still in his glass. "Sounds like you're excited about working at city hall. I'm sorry for the sarcastic comment I made at The Athena earlier, about you being overqualified. I'm sure you'll fit right in with whatever job the mayor has for you."

Nice to know he thinks I'm a competent person. "No offense taken. And thanks for the vote of confidence."

"Are you ready to go?"

She nodded, picked up her purse, and stood. Chad put a hand on the small of her back and guided her to the dark green exit door on the other side of the room. She stopped at the door and turned to face him. "Don't we have to pay the check?"

"No. My granddad owned half of this establishment."

"The part that's in town?"

Chad nodded. "And my dad has the property now."

Why am I not surprised?

Outside, the full, yellow moon shone brighter than the stars. Having lived in Chicago her entire life, Heather wasn't used to seeing this many stars in the night sky. Most of the time, she saw none at all. It was difficult to look away.

A light breeze caressed her hair as they made their way to Chad's car. She loved summer nights like this. They gave her a warm, cozy feeling. She stepped inside Chad's Lexus, and he started the engine. A moment later his cell phone pinged.

"It's a text from Officer Henderson. I told him to let me know if there was any information about the man who was found at the bottom of the stairs."

Heather stared at Chad's handsome face in anticipation. But before she could ask about Denny, he placed his hand over hers. "The guy died between eleven and one."

Her heart sank. This was around the time her aunt said she'd heard someone on the back steps. Bad news for Julia. Much worse than Chad could ever imagine. She couldn't help thinking her aunt had something to do with his death. After all, Jimmy thought she gave Denny one of her infamous shoves, whatever that meant.

"Oh no," Heather said. "May the poor man rest in peace. I only hope my aunt isn't somehow responsible."

"I hope she's not too. I mean... I'm sure she's not."

"But I have a terrible feeling that someone was behind it. Someone who wanted to get rid of this guy."

"The police are probably thinking the same way. They've taken the body to the local mortuary. Doc Willis, from the clinic, will perform a preliminary autopsy tomorrow morning to determine the cause of death. He sometimes subs as a coroner when the real coroner's not available."

"I think he's my aunt's new doctor. The one she went to see when she had her prescription refilled a few weeks ago."

If she didn't take her pills every day, Julia could get prickly. Much worse than she already was. Heather had to deal with her mood swings. It wasn't fun.

"The doc's been around ever since I was a kid," Chad said. "He was our primary care physician until my dad had a falling out with him during my mom's illness."

"I'm sorry about your mom, but my aunt seems to like him." Heather didn't know what else to say. Besides, there were other things on her mind. Worrisome things she wasn't in the mood to discuss. She suspected her aunt, or Jimmy, knew if Denny had been murdered or not, and if so, why, and probably by whom. It might have been another member of Jimmy's gang who'd followed him here. At least, it had to be someone the man knew and who knew him. But who in this town did he know except Julia and Jimmy?

<><><>

Chad drove his Lexus into the alley and parked in his usual space behind the bookstore.

The back stairs had been cordoned off with yellow police tape.

"I'm glad I saw this," Heather said. "I might have blundered out the back door in the morning on my way to City Hall."

"Tomorrow is tomorrow," Chad said, "but we still have tonight. Let me walk you upstairs, where we can have some privacy."

Heather slipped her arm through his. "What did you have in mind?"

In a few moments, they were on the top landing. Chad wrapped his arms around her and pulled her close, his hands traveling up her back and into her hair. Heather snaked her arms around his neck and raised her lips to his in anticipation.

A ruckus broke out at the bottom of the stairs, and they both turned their heads to see what it was about.

Chapter 11

AUNT Julia came stomping up the stairs with Jimmy the Horse close on her heels. "I'm telling you, Jim, it's not gonna happen!"

"Don't forget, you owe me..." His voice tapered off as Julia stopped one step before the upstairs landing. She put a hand to her chest in a gesture of surprise.

"Oh! I wasn't expecting to see you two."

Jimmy stopped on the stair beneath hers. He was so tall, he and Julia were almost equal in height now.

"Can't you people do *anything* in your own apartment?" he said.

Chad covered his mouth with his hand, but Heather could still detect the huge smile underneath. She nearly burst into laughter but bit her bottom lip to suppress it.

"We can't go up the back stairs to the attic apartment," Chad said. "The police have them cordoned off because of the incident that happened earlier today, so we came to ask Julia if we could go through her apartment to get upstairs."

Julia looked visibly relieved as she unlocked the front door. "Sure you can. Come on through."

Heather and Chad followed her into the apartment with Jimmy lagging behind. He slammed their front door shut. Heather's shoulders hitched at the loud and unexpected sound.

"Have a good night." Chad clasped Heather's hand and led her toward the back door.

"Why don't you stay and have a night cap?" Jimmy eyed Heather's long, auburn hair and form-fitting dress.

Julia set her fists on her hips. "Put your eyes back in your head, and let these people go on their way. It's late, and unlike you, we all have to get up early tomorrow morning."

Julia grabbed Jimmy's arm, turned him around, opened the front door, and propelled him out onto the landing. Then she slammed the door and locked it.

Heather came into the living room, followed by Chad. Her jaw dropped as she stared at her aunt. "That was kind of rude."

"Rude is the only thing Jimmy the Horse understands. My voice is nearly gone from trying to reason with him. But I'm so glad you two were here when we got back. You gave me the support I needed to get rid of that blowhard. Thinks he can get the best of me? We'll see about that!"

Heather put a comforting arm around her aunt's tense shoulders. "Calm down. He's gone now."

Julia chewed her lip. "Yes, but for how long?"

"I should be going too." Chad made his way to the front door. "But before I do, I think you should know, Julia, that the man at the bottom of the stairs was dead on arrival at the hospital. They're doing a preliminary autopsy on his body tomorrow to determine the cause of death."

Julia dragged her hands over her face. "Poor Denny. He was only doing his job. But it's a good thing you didn't tell me when Jimmy was here. He'll be furious. He thinks I shoved Denny down the stairs."

Heather took her arm down. "While we're on the subject, what did Jimmy mean when he said you might have given Denny one of your *infamous* shoves?"

"Oh that." Julia clicked her tongue. "Denny got fresh with me at a train station once, and I shoved him into a waiting crowd. People went down like bowling pins. Jimmy witnessed the incident. That man never forgets anything."

Heather let out a breath. "That's not so bad. I was afraid… Never mind. But if it makes you feel any better, Denny might have died from another cause."

Julia glanced at her. "Like what?"

"We'll just have to wait until after the preliminary autopsy tomorrow to find out."

"It's late," Chad said. "I really have to go."

Heather rushed up to him. "Do you think what happened today will affect the mayor's decision about hiring me?"

She'd been living on the money she'd won betting on the Kentucky Derby a couple weeks ago, but she could only stretch a dollar so far. Frugality was not one of her strong suits.

Chad gazed into her eyes. "I wish I could tell you what you want to hear, but I can't, so I'll just wish you good luck." He unlocked the door and opened it. "Night, ladies." He strolled out. Heather closed it behind him and turned the lock. This wasn't the way she'd hoped the evening would end. She would have loved to get a goodnight kiss, but her aunt put the kibosh on that.

<><><>

The morning light peeked in through the worn shade on Heather's bedroom window, and her eyes shot open as her heartbeat quickened. "What time is it?"

Exhausted after everything that happened yesterday, she'd collapsed into bed after changing into her PJs and forgotten to set an alarm. The clock on her cell phone read, *9:10 a.m.* She breathed a sigh of relief. Her mayoral office appointment wasn't until 10:15. That gave her just enough time to get dressed and drive there.

The Willows Bend Retirement Village, where her aunt was doing community service this week, sent their bus to pick Julia up at 8:00 when it dropped off some of its residents at the Willows Park Fieldhouse for morning swim classes. Then it brought her back home in the afternoon when her shift was over, so Heather didn't have to drive her this week.

She jumped out of bed and inhaled the invigorating scent of fresh coffee. That was one less thing she had do this morning. But why didn't her aunt wake her? Or did she? Now that she thought about it, she remembered being shaken earlier, but she'd rolled over and gone back to sleep.

After a quick shower, she applied her makeup, dressed in her favorite business suit, and brushed her hair. Now she was really running late, so she jammed a slice of toast into her mouth, poured hot coffee into a travel mug, and ran out the door.

Thank goodness City Hall was only six blocks away. At this time of the morning, there wasn't much traffic. She pulled into the only empty parking spot in front of the white brick, two story building. A carved, stone sign over the wooden doors read, *City Hall.* What made this building unique was the oxidized green clock attached to the west corner, similar to the one on the old Marshall Field building in downtown Chicago but on a much smaller scale. An American flag hung from a tall pole next to the front steps.

As soon as she turned off the car's engine, the queasiness started again, but she was running late, and she didn't have time to indulge it, so a few quick, deep breaths had to do as she stepped out of the car and rushed into the building.

The quiet inside was deafening. The clicking of her spiked heels on the white marble floor sounded like explosions. A large placard on the wall listed all the offices in the building in small, block lettering. The Mayor's was on the second floor.

She rushed to the elevator at the other end of the short corridor and pressed the button, checking her cell phone for the time. "Two minutes to spare."

As the elevator doors opened on the second floor, Heather nearly ran into a middle-aged woman with short, brown hair and wire-rimmed half-glasses balanced on the end of her long nose.

The woman stepped back to let Heather out. "Can I help you?"

"I have a meeting with the mayor this morning."

The woman eyed her from head to toe, and then a huge smile graced her thin, glossy lips. "You must be Miss Stanton."

"Yes, I am."

"Sylvia, isn't that coffee ready yet?" An annoyed base voice yelled out.

The woman smirked at her. "That boisterous person is Mayor Bandyk. I'm Sylvia Murphy, his administrative assistant." She waved an empty glass coffee pot in the air.

"He drinks a lot of coffee. Too much, in my opinion. Makes him jittery. I was just on my way downstairs to get more water for a fresh pot."

Heather nodded. "Pleased to meet you, Ms. Murphy."

"Just call me Sylvia. Everyone does."

Before Heather could ask where the mayor's office was located, Sylvia turned and walked a few steps back. She stuck her head into an open door. "Coffee will be ready in a few minutes, Mr. Mayor. By the way, Miss Stanton is here."

"Well, send her in." The mayor sounded annoyed.

Sylvia pointed toward the door. "You heard him." Then she scurried to catch the elevator.

Heather stepped into the mayor's office, a little apprehensive. He was irritated already, and it was only 10:30. She hoped this wasn't his usual temperament. He seemed so jovial yesterday. But then, it *was* Monday morning.

Chapter 12

HEATHER walked across the parquet floor of the large rectangular room where various photos, old and new, mostly of buildings in town, hung on the beige plaster walls. At the far end of the room, overlooking the street, the mayor's large, rosewood desk was strewn with file folders. A thirty-six-inch computer monitor stood on the right corner. Two white leather arm chairs sat in front of the desk. The town's flag and an American flag flanked it on either side.

"Come in and have a seat." He sounded encouraging.

She sat on the edge of one of the armchairs as he leaned over his desk.

"What can I do for you?"

I have to remind him? "At The Athena yesterday, you told me to be here this morning because you had a short-term job for me."

"Did I?" He tapped on his keyboard with a shaky hand and checked his computer screen. "That's right, I did. I mean, I do. It's a temporary position I just created and will only last until the mayoral election in November. You see, I'm not running again, and I don't know what staff the new mayor will decide to keep. That's why, when I heard you were interested in a short-term job, I thought you'd be the perfect candidate."

Sylvia rushed in with a coffee cup in hand and placed it on the coaster on the mayor's desk.

"Close the door on your way out," he said.

As Sylvia scurried out, he took several sips from his cup. It seemed to calm his shakes. "That's better. Now, what was I saying?"

"About the new position."

"What I'm looking for is a Project Manager to get some of my pet projects accomplished before I leave office, so the people of this town will remember me as the mayor who cared, in case I want to run again, or one of my family members wants to run in the future."

Heather smiled. "Having worked in marketing, I'm excellent at managing projects." *But politics is something I'll never understand.*

"Somehow, I knew you would be. I spoke with some of your former co-workers this morning."

Terror stuck her heart. "You spoke with my old boss?" Her shoulders dropped. *I'm sunk.*

"No, I spoke with the people who really knew you, middle management. I always get a better behavioral perspective from them. And they all told me the same thing—that your former boss had given you a raw deal."

Heather let out a sigh. It was about time someone spoke up about that situation, even though it was too late to change the outcome.

"But that's not the reason I wanted to hire you. After what you did to catch and rid this town of the undesirables, I think you have the ingenuity, fortitude, and resilience to complete the tasks I have in mind."

"I'll try not to disappoint you, Mr. Mayor."

His grin lit up his pudgy face from ear to ear. "I'm sure you won't. Sylvia will give you all the details for your first assignment and set you up with everything you need, including a laptop so you can work from home if the need arises. Otherwise, you'll be working from a small office in this building. Heck, I work from my office in The Athena most of the time."

Heather stood. "Thank you for giving me the opportunity to prove myself."

"You're entirely welcome." He picked up his office telephone and pressed a button on the base. "Sylvia, take Ms. Stanton to her new office, and get her up to speed on everything. She'll be out in a minute."

He stood and offered her his hand. "Goodbye, and don't forget I'm counting on you."

Heather shook it. "I'll do my best." She walked out the door where Sylvia was waiting in the hall.

"He made it sound like he was doing you a favor," the woman whispered.

"How do you know what he said?"

"I'm right next door. Walls are paper thin around here. Keep that in mind."

Sylvia led Heather down a short hall and unlocked the door labeled, *Store Room*. The room couldn't have measured more then eight by ten, if that. The white walls were lined with several labeled bankers boxes, making the room look even smaller. A little mahogany desk sat in the center, with a Kelly green office chair pushed under it. If there hadn't been a tall, narrow window in the corner, the room would have been in total darkness.

Sylvia went to the window and pulled up the white accordion shade. "You'll be using this room as your office. Probably not what you're used to, having worked at a big Chicago marketing firm, but then, this is a small town."

She pulled out the middle desk drawer and grabbed a laptop. "Here's your computer, to be used for business purposes only." She set it on the desk and dropped a cord on top. "It needs to be charged if you're taking it out of the office, but you can just plug it in to use for now. Once it's on, it'll be linked with the main computer, which is joined to all the other computers in the building. So you'll need to give every project you work on a separate password, or everyone will be able to access it. Same with any business emails you receive or send. Your email address is your name at the email address you got from the mayor yesterday. I.T. is working on setting you up right now."

Heather's forehead creased in confusion. "What project will I be working on?"

Sylvia went to the door and glanced out in both directions before she closed it. "Before I tell you about it, you'll have to sign a document stating that you won't reveal any confidential information you come across while you're working here, to anyone, especially not to the press, unless the mayor okays it. Read the document, sign it, and email it back to me.

What kind of project is this?

"Sure." The word nearly stuck in Heather's throat.

"Here." Sylvia dropped two keys into Heather's hand. "One is for the front door, and the other is to your door. Just as a precaution, please lock it anytime you go out. There are people wandering the halls all day, especially on the first floor where the different bureaus are located. We wouldn't want anything disappearing from your office while you're away. Would we?"

Sylvia grabbed the door handle. But Heather still had questions. "The mayor didn't mention my salary or my hours."

"You don't have any set working hours. Put in as many as you need to complete the assignment, and do it as quickly as you can. As far as your salary goes, I'll email you all that information. Got other questions? Just ask. Welcome aboard."

After she left, Heather went back to her desk. She opened the laptop and plugged it in. As she waited for it to boot up, she flipped a switch on the wall, turning on the single overhead fluorescent light, and checked out her desk drawers. Most were empty.

The computer finally booted, and she opened the email from Sylvia containing several attachments. One was the NDA, which she signed and sent back. Then she found her salary.

"Yikes." It was less than half of what she'd made as a marketing executive, and it was paid on a twice monthly basis. She hoped she'd get a raise or a bonus once she completed her first project. But she was glad to have *any* income for now.

The next attachment was her assignment. She was to put a 4th of July dance together at the old Willow's Bend Dance Hall on Saturday, July 3rd. But before she started, she'd have to submit a budget for the mayor's approval.

She sighed. A budget? She'd never done one before. That was part of her former boss's job.

As she thought about emailing Sylvia to ask for help, her cell phone rang.

She checked the screen. "Aunt Julia. Hey."

"Hi Heather. Did you get the job?"

"Yes, I did." The more important question was, 'why was her aunt calling her during the day?' "Is something wrong at the Retirement Village? Are you hurt? Are you in trouble? Did you get arrested again?"

"No. Nothing like that. The senior citizen's bus has a fuel line leak, but they're working on it. So you have to pick me up this afternoon, around four. Is that a problem?"

"No. I'm pretty sure I can make it."

"Thanks, I'll be waiting in the game room on the first floor. See you later."

Heather clicked off the call but thought twice about sending the email. This was better handled in person.

Chapter 13

Heather found the mayor's administrative assistant at her desk in the small office next to the mayor's. She knocked on the open door frame. "Hi. I hate to bother you, but I have a few questions."

Sylvia turned away from her computer screen. "It's okay. What do you want to know?"

Heather hesitated before telling her she'd never created a budget before, so she started with a noncommittal question. "First of all, where can I get coffee?"

"You don't want to drink the coffee here. It's sludge, but that's the way the mayor likes it. You can always bring your own coffee maker and make coffee in your office." She picked up her tall, paper cup and flashed it at Heather. "Personally, I get my morning cappuccino from the coffee house across the street."

"Thanks. I think I'll bring mine from home. It's less expensive that way. And another thing..." She brought her voice down to a whisper so the mayor wouldn't hear. "The mayor wants me to submit a budget for the project I'm working on, and I've never done one before."

Sylvia walked to the door and closed it. "I'll send you an email on how to create a basic project budget so you can see what goes into making it and how to calculate one."

"Thanks. I was a little nervous about it."

Sylvia placed a hand on Heather's shoulder. "Don't worry. At first glance, the whole budget thing might seem intimidating, but eventually you'll realize all you need to do is to iron out the plan."

Heather let out a breath. "That makes me feel a lot better."

Sylvia was clearly in charge of more important things in the mayor's office than just keeping his coffee mug filled.

"Have you worked here long?" Heather asked.

"I came when Mayor Bandyk was first elected, twelve years ago. But unfortunately, this will be my last few months. After the November election, when the new administration replaces his, I'm sure they'll want to bring in their own people."

Heather couldn't help but ask. "Why isn't the mayor running again?"

"Says he's through with politics and wants to open another restaurant. This time in Chicago. But I think it's because he's got Parkinson's. Haven't you noticed the tremor in his right hand?"

"I thought it was the jitters from drinking too much coffee."

"That's what he wants people to think. And Harrison Kane is taking advantage of it by running for mayor unopposed in November. In my opinion, he's a gangster. No one wants to go up against him. He'll ruin this town."

"But I heard from Christine Talan that he owns a successful garden center and florist."

"I think it's a front. I don't know all the facts, but from what I hear, he's been working real hard to lobby for a casino to be built on Bleaker Street. Mayor Bandyk is hoping this dance hall project will be a huge success so the residents will vote the casino idea down."

Makes me glad I'll be leaving in November but sad for the people who have to live here.

Heather left Sylvia deep in thought as she strolled back to her own office. As she stared down at the keys in her hand she bumped into someone.

He stumbled, and a tight, sweaty hand grabbed her arm. The short, middle-aged man whom she recognized as the mayor's accountant, eyed her from head to toe.

"I beg your pardon," he said in a scathing tone.

"I'm so sorry. Are you hurt?"

He gave her a silent, shifty-eyed stare. Then his gaze shot to the cell phone in his hand.

"Are you okay?" she asked again.

Marty, she thought his name was, nodded several times and touched his lips with a trembling hand. "Have to go. I'm late for an important meeting."

He rushed off as if he was being chased by the devil himself.

Heather made her way back to her office. *What a squirrely man. Makes me nervous.* She unlocked the door, walked in, and glanced around the stuffy room.

Walking to the window, she wasted ten minutes trying to figure out how to get it open before it finally dawned on her that it didn't open upward, but outward. She took a deep breath of air, only to pull her head inside when her nostrils filled with smoke.

She coughed. "Why is it so smoky out there?"

She shut the window and called Sylvia, still coughing. "There must be a fire behind the building. I smell wood burning, and smoke is coming in through my open window."

"Don't panic." Sylvia chuckled. "That's just the deli down the street. They smoke their salmon on Monday mornings. Covers up the smell of the garbage trucks parked out back. Monday is also garbage pickup day."

Heather scrunched her face. She'd have to remember not to open her window on Mondays. She could see why the mayor worked out of the office at the back of his restaurant.

Sylvia continued. "The air conditioning should clear your office of the smoke in a few minutes."

"Okay, hopefully that works. Thanks, Sylvia." Heather ended the call and sat at the desk in her tiny office, putting some heavy thought into her project. She'd need a comprehensive list of things to do and things she needed to purchase.

After a morning of concentrating on how to make a budget, she sat back in her chair facing the large, circular wall clock above her screen. Nearly twelve-thirty. Heather's stomach rumbled. She'd only eaten a quick slice of toast for breakfast, and she'd finished the thermos of coffee she'd brought in, around eleven.

She stopped at Sylvia's office on the way out. "I'm going home to grab some lunch. Can I bring you back anything?"

"It's very kind of you to offer, but no thanks. I always bring my lunch and eat at my desk. There's a break room in the basement with a refrigerator, a microwave, and loads of vending machines. There are a few tables with chairs if you care to bring your own lunch."

"Thanks," Heather said. "But I only live a few blocks away."

After locking up, she walked out the front door of City Hall, and a wave of oppressive heat took her breath away.

It was like walking into a five-hundred-degree oven. The sign in front of the First National Bank of Willows Bend across the street said the temperature was 95 degrees. She could barely touch her car door handle to open it. She slipped off her lightweight suit jacket, flung it onto the passenger seat, and switched on the air full blast.

As Heather waited for the car to cool, the mayor's accountant ran out of the building, straight to the forest green Jeep Cherokee parked two cars down from her. *He said he had an important meeting. He must be late.*

She headed home to grab her lunch and to find out the autopsy results on Denny Serrano.

Chapter 14

HEATHER pulled her rental car up next to Chad's Lexus in the alley behind the bookstore. The police tape still cordoned off the steps to her apartment. She managed to squeeze behind it and slipped into the back room of the bookstore. Chad and Ashley were eating their lunches.

"I'm sorry. I didn't mean to disturb you while you're eating. I just wanted to find out about the autopsy results."

"It's okay." Ashley motioned to an empty chair at the small table. "If you haven't eaten, why don't you join us? There's plenty. Chad always orders too much Chinese takeout. Besides, we're dying to find out how your job's going at the mayor's office."

"Thanks, I'd love to join you." Heather plopped down on the chair and stepped out of her white stilettos.

The cold tile floor brought her body temperature down a few degrees and soothed her aching feet. Since her job wasn't one where she had to look formal, she planned to change into her sandals before going back.

As she took one of the egg rolls and piled her paper plate with rice and shrimp in lobster sauce, she explained her first assignment as, "just some computer work right now." What else could she say after she'd signed that agreement not to discuss her work with anyone?

"Sounds pretty dull," Ashley said, between bites.

"It's not so bad," Heather said. "Actually, it's just a small part of the job. But I can't talk about the rest until I get the okay from the mayor's office."

Chad tilted his head. "It sounds official."

She gave them a smile that reeked of self-assurance. What she really wanted to say was, *This appears to be a test to see if I can get a job done on time and stick to a budget.*

They ate the rest of their meal in silence, until Heather broke it. "I never got a chance to ask if they released the autopsy report yet?"

"Sam Henderson texted me a little while ago," Chad said. "The preliminary cause of death was a broken neck, which may have been caused by a fall down the stairs as he landed on the concrete patio outside our back door. He had some bruising on his head, but they haven't determined what caused it."

Heather swallowed hard. "You mean like he might have been hit with a blunt object?" *Like my aunt's baseball bat? If they find his DNA on it, Julia's sunk.*

"They don't know," Chad continued. "They won't determine that until they do a full autopsy."

"But they'll probably do that soon," Ashley added.

Heather's stomach locked. She couldn't eat another bite. Slowly getting out of her chair, she slipped into her shoes, dropped her paper plate in the trash, and made her way to the door. "Thanks for lunch. I really have to get back to work if I intend to complete the first part of my new assignment."

She opened the back door, right into a web of police tape. "Oh, I'll go out the front."

Chad scrunched his eyes. "Are you okay?"

"Sure. Why shouldn't I be?" Heather rushed out into the scorching noontime sun. Once on the sidewalk, she had to make a decision—should she call the retirement village to question her aunt or wait until this afternoon?

There was no reason to upset Julia right now. There would be plenty of time for that later. Heather had promised to pick her up around four, and in the meantime, maybe a determination would be made on what caused Denny's head bruises, and it might not concern her at all.

Heather headed to the door of her apartment to get out of the heat. She needed to change into a short sleeved blouse and low-heeled sandals for what she wanted to do.

Chapter 15

HER claustrophobic office was not a place Heather looked forward to spending the afternoon, even if it was cool inside. She filled a large thermos with ice water and left to go to the dance hall to see what categories she needed to add to her budget.

But first, she'd have to stop at City Hall and get the keys. She texted Sylvia who told her they were in the building commissioner's office.

Heather made her way to the first floor and checked the names on the closed doors. The first door she came to was: *Dana Gray, Building Commissioner.* She knocked, and the door was opened by a petite blond. From the light wrinkles around her eyes, she looked to be about ten years older than Heather, maybe in her early forties.

She gave Heather a bright smile with astonishingly white teeth. "Can I help you?"

"Hi, I'm looking for Dana Gray."

"That's me. What can I do for you?" She wasn't exactly what Heather had pictured for a Building Commissioner.

"I'm—"

"You don't have to tell me," Dana interrupted. "You're Heather Stanton. I know who you are. I'm pretty sure the whole town knows you by now. You're working for the mayor, aren't you?"

"Yes, I am. It's nice to meet you, Ms. Gray."

"It's my pleasure. Call me Dana. What can I do to help?"

"I need the keys to um..." She checked for the address on her business cell. "2510 North Bleaker Street."

"Oh, you mean the old Willows Bend Dance Hall?"

Heather nodded. "That's the place."

"Just a minute. I figured you might need those keys, so I put them aside. At the mayor's request, I had some of my people check out the building structure last week to see if it was sound. The building inspector gave it a thorough going over. In case you're wondering, everything's in good shape... on the outside."

She handed Heather the keys.

"That's a load off my mind. Thanks."

"Good luck with the project. If you can get that old place ready for a dance before the Fourth of July, I'll give you a lot of credit."

Guess this project wasn't a secret after all. It's probably all over town by now.

Dana's smile turned into a frown. "That is, if you can convince anybody to go there."

Heather understood what she was talking about. Bleaker wasn't the nicest street in town. She'd gone to the pawn shop there with her aunt when they first arrived and found the entire area to be extremely run down.

<><><>

Bleaker was a few blocks over from the Franklin House Hotel near the railroad tracks and on the same street as the Willow's Bend Medical Clinic, but where she needed to go was in the opposite direction from the well-kept part of town.

She drove past tall weeds, boarded up storefronts, and the whitewashed Salvation Army store standing out like a beacon of trust and hope amid the shabbiness surrounding it.

Down the street, the door to the pawn shop, with its flashing lights and glittery window display, opened, and Jimmy the Horse walked out, looking like he really didn't have much to pawn. All her aunt's gambling buddies were like that—either flush or broke.

The man had the time-worn face of someone who drank too much. He waved his hands in the air like he was trying to flag her down, but she looked away and kept driving.

"I'm not getting involved with my aunt's problems. I've got enough of my own right now."

Several blocks down, on the corner, was a hardwood bench faded to a dull pink from years of wear. It looked as if it might have been part of a bus stop at one time.

A half block behind the bench stood a sturdy-looking red brick building with a black peaked roof, and the numbers 2510 in tarnished gold lettering, barely recognizable on the outside wall. A washed-out wooden sign over the front double doors read, *Willows Bend Dance Hall.*

She pulled into a parking spot in the block-long, black-topped lot and got out of her car to survey the area.

High grass and overgrown bushes surrounded the building, nearly covering the graffiti on the side walls.

Several large rectangular glass windows were boarded up with wood slats. The same for the back door.

At least the building itself was solid. The bricks looked good, but they could use some tuck-pointing. That might be easily done with the right contractor.

She made a note to find local contractors who were available to clean graffiti, do landscaping, and tuck-pointing at a good price. She'd add those categories to her budget.

Heather pulled the keys from her purse, turned the lock, and went in.

The large the main room was long and rectangular with a tall peaked ceiling held up by thick wooden beams. The old boards on the large windows let in enough light to make out two dozen or more small covered tables in a grouping near the front. The chairs had been pushed over to the other side of the enormous room. A low-rise bandstand stood at the back.

Heather came up to the first small table covered in a white sheet and pulled it off. Dust flew around the room. She waved it away and gazed at the solid mahogany round table, a little worse for the wear. Then she went across the room and did the same to one of the chairs. She plopped down on the red velvet seat. Still comfortable but a little musty smelling. She added a note to have the chairs cleaned and buy table cloths.

The dark green walls needed a good coat of paint in a light color to brighten up the room, and the wood floors needed to be refinished. She added those categories to her budget.

On her way to the back room, Heather glanced at her cell in the hope Chad might have texted with more information from the coroner's office about Denny's cause of death. No messages. She frowned. *It would be great to give Aunt Julia some good news for a change.*

It was nearly four o'clock when Heather closed and locked the dance hall door and headed to the retirement village. She arrived just after four and found her aunt sitting in the game room at a small square table with three village residents whom she recognized as Eloise Brown and brothers, Hank and Len Hutchinson.

She'd met them before when she came to pick up her aunt. The three were eager to play the horses. She hoped Aunt Julia wasn't still acting as their bookie. While there was a slight probability she was, Julia assured her she'd only take their money when she had a really hot tip on a horse. It was still unethical, but Heather had no control over her aunt's actions.

As she neared the table, Julia shuffled the deck of cards in her hand.

She came up behind her aunt. "Playing poker?"

Julia could take these poor elderly residents for everything they had, and they wouldn't have a clue how she did it. She never let her emotions show on her face, which made her an excellent card player, but Heather often found it frustrating.

Julia set the deck down on the table and let out a breath. "No." She glanced up at Heather and smiled. "Just doing a little Cartomancy."

Eloise nodded. "Hi Heather. Your aunt just told my fortune."

Hank waved his hello, and his watery blue eyes met hers. "I don't believe any of it."

Len shook his gray head like he was shaking off Hank's words. "My brother doesn't believe in much of anything."

"Well, you may not believe it," Eloise said, "but we sure had a lot of fun today. And it took our minds off of what happened Sunday morning. That poor man found in the alley behind the book store. It's all anyone in this place can talk about. They've been speculating about what he was doing there."

"I think he was a burglar," Hank said. "Maybe he was going to burgle Julia's apartment when he thought she might be at church."

"Naw," his brother contradicted. "He was too well-dressed to be a burglar. Didn't you notice those fancy shoes he had on when we saw him in The Athena eating breakfast on Sunday morning?"

"Was he alone?" Heather asked.

"No, he was with some really tall guy, new in town. And Johnny Tanner from the off-track betting place, along with Sylvia, the mayor's assistant."

"Why would Tanner and the mayor's assistant be with them?" Julia asked.

"I can answer that." Eloise winked. "Sylvia and Johnny Tanner have been dating for the past couple of years, and rumor has it, the dead guy spent a lot of time at the off-track betting place, so that's probably where he knew Johnny from."

Len looked at Heather. "The reason we noticed the dead guy, I mean, before he was dead, was because my son-in-law wore a pair of shoes like he had on when he and my daughter came to visit. And they ain't cheap."

"Did you tell the police you saw him in the restaurant that morning?" Heather asked.

"The police haven't questioned us yet," Hank said. "But we'll tell them when they do."

Julia slid the card deck back into its box, dropped it in the large, green leather valise she called a purse, and waved at the three elderly residents. "See you tomorrow."

Eloise waved back. "We'll be waiting."

<><><>

As soon as they got into the car, Heather asked, "Are you telling fortunes, now?"

"I told a few this afternoon, just for fun."

"Telling fortunes can get you into a lot of trouble."

Julia laughed. "You got that right. But I'm careful. Whatever the cards tell me could fit into anyone's life at any given time, if you know how to interpret them and are any good at reading people."

"I have to admit, you're very good at reading people."

"Most people, yes. But there are a few exceptions, like The Horse. Why do you suppose Jimmy went to The Athena for breakfast on Sunday morning with Denny when the hotel puts out a fabulous Sunday Brunch?"

"All I can think of," Heather said, "is because they were looking for you and thought you might be having breakfast at the restaurant. Or someone told them you were there. What I can't figure out is why Sylvia would want to date Johnny Tanner. He's so rough around the edges, and she's so refined."

"Love truly is blind," Julia said a moment before her cell phone rang. "It's Christine Talan. I haven't heard from her in a week, ever since George came home from his last trucking job."

She answered the call. "Hello... Yes. Oh, really? Great. No, we don't have any dinner plans for tonight." She glanced at Heather. "Do we?"

At the moment, Heather wasn't sure. She still had hopes Chad would ask her, but she said, "No."

She could always cancel if he called, even at the last minute.

"Okay, we'll see you at six." Julia ended the call and turned to Heather. "George is out of town for a few days. Christine is making her special lasagna and garlic bread."

It was another one of Heather's favorite dishes. "Sounds delicious."

<><><>

The fact that Chad lived next door to the Talans had nothing to do with Heather's decision to eat dinner there. After all, a free meal was a free meal, at least until she could get her first paycheck from City Hall, which wouldn't be for another two weeks. And Christine was an exceptional cook. She'd have to take lessons from her. Aunt Julia wasn't much help with the cooking, although she did make incredible coffee.

Heather turned into the driveway of the Talan house, an architectural copy of the Willow's mansion next door, but on a much smaller scale and without the swimming pool. The Talan house was pushed back on the lot, so the grassy front yard, mowed to within an inch of its life, stretched all the way to the street. There were no sidewalks here in what Aunt Julia called the *ritzy part* of town.

Christine opened the front door before they got out of the car. She rushed up to them, a warm, inviting smile on her glossy lips. She was about the same age as Aunt Julia, in her mid-fifties, and wore her dark brown hair short with bangs that flattered her heart-shaped face.

"You're right on time," she said. "I just took the garlic bread out of the oven."

"How did you know we were out here?" Heather asked.

"George has this house wired for everything. He gets nervous with me being home alone when he's away. Especially on nights I'm working at the hotel. He set up security cameras so I can see what's going on in the front, the back, on the sides of the house, and in the garage. And I can see it all from my cell phone. Remind me to show you my secure room downstairs sometime. But right now... let's eat before everything gets cold."

Heather handed her the bottle of Merlot she'd picked up on the way.

Christine read the label. "Thanks. That was thoughtful of you. We can drink this with dinner, along with the bottle Chad brought."

Heather's heart fluttered. "Is he here too?"

"Yes, he and Ashley got here about ten minutes ago. And, of course, Makki." Christine leaned in close to Heather and Julia. "Don't mention Miklos, or Ashley'll start crying again."

Heather was dying to know what happened to the once happy couple, but she wouldn't dare ask, especially at dinner. Ashley might confide in her later.

Chad's downturned lips turned into a grin when their gazes met. "I didn't know you'd be here. But I'm glad you came."

Heather was glad she came too.

Ashley waved her fingers at them in acknowledgement, her lovely dark eyes rimmed in red.

After Heather and her aunt were seated, Christine served the lasagna and garlic bread. Ashley downed her entire glass of wine and poured herself another before picking at the lasagna on her plate. Chad finished his slice before Heather could eat half of hers. Then he helped himself to another from the serving dish. The only noise was the clicking of forks on plates.

Ashley let out a loud sigh. "It's okay. You can all talk. Don't mind me. I'm just not very good company tonight." She gulped her wine and stared at her plate.

Makki jumped up on the end of the table where no one sat and padded around until he found a spot he wanted to occupy. He sat on his haunches, staring at everyone as they ate.

Chad waved his hand at the cat. "Makki, get down. You've already been fed."

Makki gave out a loud meow, sounding seriously perturbed. He walked in a circle and finally jumped off the table.

Chad turned to his sister. "Tell me why we had to bring the cat here tonight."

"Because I find his presence comforting. And besides, Christine doesn't mind, do you?"

Christine waved her fork. "Not at all. I love having Makki here. Why do you think I keep a litter box?" Then she turned her attention to Julia.

"You'll never guess who's been staying at the hotel."

Without hesitation, Julia said, "Denny Serrano and Jimmy, the Horse, Marlucci?"

Christine's jaw dropped. "Yes. Although Denny showed up first, and then about a week after he arrived, The Horse, as you call him, joined him. I saw the two of them together on more than one occasion, and they appeared to be as thick as thieves."

"That's just who they were," Julia murmured under her breath.

"Anyway," Christine continued. "They both asked about you. But I didn't tell them anything. The only thing I said was that you stayed at the hotel for a while, and then you checked out without leaving a forwarding address."

She turned to Heather. "And by the way, your ex-boyfriend, Jack Steele, checked in the same day as Mr. Marlucci. I would have given you a heads up that he was here, but I didn't want to upset you. And I thought if he couldn't find you, he might just go away. Anyway, I think they must have both come in on the 3:40 train from Chicago that afternoon."

Heather nodded. "Probably."

"Thanks for being a good friend," Julia said.

"You're welcome." Christine took a sip of wine and grabbed another piece of garlic bread. "Now it's your turn. How do you know these men?"

Julia explained a bit of her history with the two men as they all finished their drinks.

"I knew it!" Christine leaned in closer to Julia. "Those guys looked like they were up to no good. New people always make me suspicious, especially when they ask a lot of questions about my friends."

Chapter 16

"SINCE Heather and Chad already know everything," Julia said, "I can tell you the rest."

Ashley's jaw dropped as she listened to Julia's story. It must have taken her mind off her problems, because her intense gaze never left Julia's face as she absent-mindedly chewed a few bites of food.

At the end, Julia leaned back in her chair. "I have to find a way to get rid of Jimmy for good. If he stays here, I know he'll make it look like I killed Denny. If he can't do that, then he'll formulate a plan in that sneaky brain of his to get back at me for turning him in to the Feds. And there's no walking away from this situation like I usually do, because I'm stuck here with that community service hanging over my head." Julia stabbed at a large piece of lasagna.

Christine stood and picked up her empty plate. "You could always bump him off and make it look like an accident."

Heather snorted and covered her smile with a napkin.

Julia shrugged. "It may be my only out." She smirked.

Chad shook his head. "Surely you can come up with something short of homicide to rid yourself of this man's attentions, Julia."

She downed the little wine that was left in her glass. "I haven't come up with a thing yet, and I've been racking my brain for the past two days."

Heather's gaze went to her aunt. "I've seen you get out of tougher situations than this. I'm sure if we all think about your problem, we can come up with a solution."

"As your partner in crime-solving," Christine said. "I'll be glad to help you any way I can." She clasped her hands together. "I only hope George doesn't ever find out some of the things we've done while he was away."

Heather picked up the dirty silverware from the table and followed Christine into the kitchen, where she put it in the sink alongside the soiled dishes. On the counter stood a full coffee pot and a huge, obviously homemade, apple pie.

"The lasagna and the garlic bread were delicious," Heather said.

"Thanks. I'm glad you enjoyed them. You can take home the leftovers. I usually make enough for the entire week so I don't have to cook, but now that George is away, I have loads of it. That's why I invited everyone to dinner."

"I'd be glad to take some home." Heather set a hand on Christine's shoulder. "But there's one other thing I wanted to say. Please don't let my aunt's problems come between you and your husband."

Christine picked up the coffee pot. "What George doesn't know won't hurt him. Now I'll tell *you* something. Before your aunt came to town, I was bored out of my skull. Oh, I have my kids and my grandkids, but they all live out of town, and they don't really have much time for us anymore. Julia's brought some excitement into my life. And I'll tell you one good thing that's come of this, George has stopped taking me for granted."

A sense of relief washed over Heather. "That's good to hear. I'm sorry to say my Aunt Julia tends to bring out either the best or the worst in people."

"I agree." Christine headed toward the dining room, coffee pot in hand. "Would you please bring in the pie?"

The smell of the fresh baked pie reminded Heather of the good-times at home when she was a child. Her mother liked to make pies too.

As Christine poured the coffee, Heather set the pie on the table and went back to her seat, catching the last words of what her aunt was saying.

"... but the cards might reveal something."

"Are you into Tarot?" Christine asked.

Julia shook her head. "No. Cartomancy."

"What's that?"

"Unlike Tarot, I read the past, present, and future with a regular deck of playing cards. Every card in a standard deck is credited with a certain meaning. You present your question to the cards, then pull out three cards from the deck."

"Do you think it could help with my problem?" Ashley asked.

Julia's forehead wrinkled. "I don't know if it will help or make things worse. But I'll be glad to do a reading for you, if you like."

Ashley sucked in a breath. "Here and now? Because I need an answer tonight."

Julia studied Ashley's large, long-lashed, tear-stained eyes for a few moments. "Yes, I think you're in a good state of mind for a reading." She checked something on her cell phone. "And you're in luck. There will be a new moon tonight, which is always a good sign. But you don't want other people around..." She glanced at

Chad, "who could project their own feelings onto your reading."

"Where do you suggest we do it?" Ashley asked.

"We need a place that's calm and supportive, without a lot of clutter."

Christine raised a finger. "I know. How about the play room I made for our kids when they were small? You and Chad used to play in there too."

Chad and Heather followed them out of the dining room and down a long hallway. Christine opened the door at the end to reveal a large, airy, rectangular room. She pulled the white window drapes aside, and the yellow rays of the setting sun brought the Disney-patterned wallpaper to life.

Ashley wheeled her chair around, inspecting the old toys on the shelves at eye level. "Some of the happiest days of my life were spent in this room."

"Then I guess it will do." Julia pointed to the corner. "We can use that table. Chad, would you please put it in the middle of the room, along with one of those wooden chairs?"

"Sure." He picked up the table and set it down where Julia had indicated.

"Oh no," Christine said. "That won't do. I'm turning the table..." She pushed the light piece of furniture in the other direction. "So the sun won't shine in your eyes."

"That's it!" Julia gave Christine a quick hug. "You're a genius. You've just planted the seed of an idea in my mind on how to get rid of Jimmy the Horse. Hopefully, for good."

Christine's jaw dropped. "I did?"

"Yes, but I have to figure out the best way to do it, and that may take some time."

"I'll be glad to help," Christine said.

"Thanks. It's going to be a project, and I may need all the help I can get. But right now…" She searched her purse and pulled out her deck of playing cards. She slid the cards out of their old, worn box and shuffled them. Then fanning the cards out in her hand, she blew on them from left to right. After a moment, she closed the deck, placed it on the table, and knocked on it three times.

"Why did you do that?" Ashley asked.

"I was cleansing the cards. Now they're ready."

Chad glanced at Heather. "Your aunt amazes me sometimes."

"That's one word for it." Heather said. "You never know what she'll do next."

Julia glanced at the others. "If everyone other than Ashley will kindly leave, I can get started on her reading."

Chapter 17

On the drive home, Heather said, "Ashley looked happy when she came out of the play room after her card reading. She even ate dessert."

"She was definitely in a much better mood."

"Is it okay if I ask what her problem was? I mean, it's not a secret, is it?"

A car horn beeped from behind. Heather hit the gas and continued driving down Main Street at a little over the 30-mph speed limit.

"I think it would be okay to tell you. She didn't swear me to secrecy," Julia said. "This morning, two young women came into the book store. One, a tall blonde, who Ashley recognized as Miklos's former girlfriend, Franny and the other a short, stout brunette, who she knew as Franny's friend from high school. They spent some time browsing the book shelves. When they got to the front of the store, Heather heard some of their conversation. The blonde was home for the summer from the U of I, where she was studying to get her MBA. After about an hour, the blonde bought a book on architecture, and they left. Ashley recalled Miklos telling her he was a wannabe architect."

Heather turned the corner for home. "So what's her problem?"

"That's where it gets a bit sticky. Miklos called Ashley a few hours later and cancelled their dinner date for tonight because some personal business came up and said he would call her some other time for a date. She put two and two together, and..."

Heather pulled the car into her usual parking space behind the bookstore. "He said he'd call her some other time, when they've been seeing each other every night for the past three weeks? I can understand how she could come to the conclusion he was seeing someone else."

"It's too bad, since Ashley's very much in love with him."

"Did the reading help with her problem?"

"I hope it did, but it was me who gave her my wisest advice, along with the cards. Christine told me Ashley had become extremely insecure after her accident, so I was prepared for what to tell her. The first card Ashley drew was the queen of hearts. It actually represents a blonde woman, but I couldn't tell her that. She might have associated it with the girl who was in her store this morning. So I told her it indicated that she's a woman of rare beauty. And being in a wheelchair has had no effect on that, or her intelligence, her sharp wit, or her sweet disposition. Plus, I told her she won't be in that contraption much longer, and her life will get back to normal."

"You don't know that, Aunt Julia. From what Chad tells me, even her doctors aren't sure."

"I just wanted to gave her some incentive to work harder at walking again. Otherwise, losing Miklos might cause her to give up. You know what it's like when your heart's been crushed, and you feel like you're worth less than nothing?"

Heather nodded. "Oh yes." *I've been there*. "It's very easy to become depressed."

Julia raised a knowing eyebrow. "Next, she picked the Jack of Spades, which represents an immature person with black hair. I told her it meant she'll realize a handsome man with black hair she's closely associated with is immature and can't help being a womanizer. She didn't take that news well."

"I wouldn't either," Heather said.

"And finally, the third card she picked was the five of hearts, which means there's jealousy in her life. And I reminded her that jealousy is a two-way street. All at once, her sad eyes perked up. She's probably making plans to make Miklos jealous, right now."

"Did you manipulate those cards so she'd pick the ones you wanted?" Heather asked.

Julia grabbed the car door handle. "I needed something to turn Ashley's frown into a smile." A moment later, she stepped out of the car. "Let's go upstairs. My brain isn't finished reconnoitering about my own problem."

Heather always got nervous when her aunt used outmoded words like, reconnoitering. It usually meant trouble was brewing.

"Now that I've decided what I should do," Julia continued as they trudged up the stairs, "I have to work on my plan to rid myself of a bad *horse*. But first, I have to solve the case of who killed Denny Serrano and why."

Heather trailed her into the apartment. She stepped out of her shoes, leaving them at the door. "Aunt Julia, why don't you let the police handle the Denny Serrano case? You don't have to get involved."

Julia sucked in a breath. "Of course I do. Don't you realize that if the police interview Jimmy first, he's going to make it sound like I killed Denny? He might have already gotten a plan together to frame me for Denny's murder."

"I don't think he'd do that," Heather said.

"Oh, my dear niece, you have a lot to learn about men. Especially the kind with whom I was formerly associated."

<><><>

A continuous sharp knocking on the front door woke Heather at seven the next morning. Just about the time her alarm was set to go off. And a few seconds later, it did. She jumped out of bed as Julia rushed out of the bathroom with her face half made up.

"Who the heck's at the door this early?" they said simultaneously.

Heather slipped into her robe on the way to answer it. "Who's there?" she yelled out.

"Police!"

Heather looked at her aunt with wide eyes. "What did you do, now?"

Julia shook her head and shrugged.

The knocking continued.

Julia shoved her blouse into her slacks, ran a hand over her hair, and opened the door.

Officer Sam Henderson stood before them in full uniform. He took off his cap. "Morning ladies."

Julia glared at him. "What could you possibly want at this hour of the morning?"

The officer's eyebrows nearly touched in a look of annoyance.

Heat flushed Heather's cheeks. "She means, what can we do for you?"

"I know it's early, but I wanted to inform you, the forensics team is examining your back steps along with the landing. I didn't want you to panic in case you heard noises or people talking out there."

"Thank you. That was very thoughtful." Heather started to push the door closed.

"And one more thing," Officer Henderson's muffled voice said from the other side of the door.

She stopped and opened it again.

"Detective Lindsey would like to see you both at the station some time today for questioning about the murder of Dennis Serrano."

Julia looked over Heather's shoulder at the officer. "Can you tell me if the detective has already questioned his associate, a man named James Marlucci?"

"How do you know James Marlucci was an associate of Dennis Serrano?"

"Oh," Julia said, probably sorry she mentioned it. "You hear things around town. Christine Talan, the hotel clerk, said the two of them were as thick as thieves."

"When did she tell you that?"

Heather felt it was best to clarify. "We had dinner at her house last night. Please tell the detective we'll stop by the station house to see him after work today."

"I can't go," Julia said.

The officer's flattened lips said he wasn't happy with this answer. "Why not?"

"I'm busy," Julia answered. "I'll come by another time. Maybe tomorrow."

"Fine." He put his cap back on. "I'll tell him."

Heather closed the door and turned on her aunt. "Don't surprise me with things before I've even had my morning coffee. What plans? Why can't you come to the station with me after work today?"

Julia sauntered toward the kitchen. "I was invited to be a player in a Tuesday night card game, held by my three friends at the retirement village. Eloise has been looking for a new partner ever since Esther Kwinn died a couple weeks ago."

"Yes, that was sad. But what card game are they playing? I know it can't be poker, since there's a 'no gambling' rule at the retirement village." Heather's stomach clenched.

Julia put a hand up. "Relax. It's only Pinochle. You don't play partners in poker. But it isn't at the village. My friends don't like playing cards in the game room. It's hard to concentrate when other residents are kibitzing you all evening."

She sauntered into the kitchen. "Besides, I'm not a resident, and while it's not against the rules for me to play there, it *is* frowned upon. My friends play at a place in town that lets them use their spare room for a few hours on Tuesday evenings, thanks to a grant by Chad's grandfather. Of course, it means I'll have to eat dinner at four o'clock. We'll leave right from the Village. It's Eloise's turn to drive this week, and she doesn't like to drive after dark, so the game will end around nine. And she'll drop me off here."

"Once they play cards with you, they may not invite you to play again. So try not to win every game if you want them to remain your friends."

Julia tsked. "As if..."

"Do you and your partner get a prize for winning?"

"Probably nothing but the satisfaction of knowing we've racked up the most points."

Heather crossed her fingers. She hoped the evening turned out to be nothing more than a few games of Pinochle. But with Julia, she could never be sure.

Chapter 18

"Is this room getting smaller?" Heather glared at the boxes stacked along the wall next to her desk. There were at least a dozen more than yesterday. "As if it's not tight enough in here."

She called Sylvia and asked if anyone besides herself had a key to her office, because boxes were suddenly appearing out of nowhere.

Sylvia laughed. "Besides the mayor, I have a key, also the Town Clerk. Just an FYI, we'll be storing more boxes there on a temporary basis. Everyone's cleaning out files and entering the information on their computers. This building is attempting to go paperless. Please try to ignore the boxes for now. I've called a paper shredding service. They should be here on Friday to clear them all away."

This is the strangest office I've ever worked in. Heather chalked it up to small-town life and went back to sorting through the estimates for the work she wanted done on the dance hall. She tried to stay focused, but she kept getting distracted by thoughts about reporting to Detective Lindsey at the station later today.

What *would* she tell him about the events of Sunday afternoon? What *could* she tell him that he wouldn't take out of context to make her aunt look guilty? What *should* she tell him to avoid prosecution for withholding evidence?

On the drive to the station that afternoon, a tension headache began at the back of her neck. She made a pit stop at *The Fudge Shop* and bought an entire pound of her favorite dark chocolate fudge with walnuts. She set the white bag on the passenger's seat and continued driving while munching on a large square.

I wish my aunt was here. She should have rescheduled this questioning so they'd be able to do it together. Julia was the only person she knew who could remain calm when others around her were panicking.

I, on the other hand, am a total pushover. I'll just blurt everything out.

The detective would walk all over her and twist her words around.

Heather turned her car into the police lot and pulled into a parking spot at the back. She sat and stared at the red brick building, trying to make some sense of her jumbled thoughts from the past few days, while finishing off the chocolate fudge chunk in her hand.

Detective Lindsey came out of the station and headed to his car. As he drove past, she ducked under the dashboard and hoped he didn't recognize her rental.

"Looks like he's in a hurry. I wonder where he's off to?" She breathed a sigh of relief. "I'll call him later and reschedule so Aunt Julia can come with me."

As Heather put her car in drive, her cell rang. She closed her eyes. *Please don't let this be my aunt with some major problem.* A moment later, she glanced at the screen. Ashley Willows' name came up from her contact list. *Thank goodness.*

"Hello."

"Hi Heather. Are you busy right now?"

"As a matter of fact, I'm free."

"Good. Can you come to the bookstore? I need to talk to you about something."

Heather had to wonder if this had anything to do with what Julia told Ashley during her card reading last night. "I'll be there in ten."

<><><>

As Heather opened the old oak door of the bookstore with its oval etched glass window, the bell tinkled, and she walked into the comforting scent of old and new books, but no Makki came to welcome her.

Heather walked to the back of the store. "Ashley, are you here?"

A moment later, the hum of Ashley's wheelchair approached. "I'm so glad you could come."

Heather turned as the chair came to a stop in front of her. "Are you alone in the store right now?"

"I am. Chad took Makki to the vet."

"I was wondering why he didn't greet me when I came in." That sounded like she meant Chad. "I mean the cat, not your brother. Anyway, I hope it's nothing serious."

"No. Just Makki's annual checkup. But now that Chad's not listening to our conversation, I can talk freely. I'd like to ask you a favor."

"Anything for you, Ash. You've been so kind to us since we got stuck… I mean, we ended up having to stay in town."

"I know what you mean," Ashley said. "Willows Bend isn't where I wanted to end up either. But I'm here now, and like you, I'm stuck here for a while. I don't know how long it'll be before I can walk again. And when I do, there'll be only one thing holding me here."

"The bookstore?"

"No."

"Your brother?"

"God no." Ashley gazed at her as if she was crazy. "I mean Miklos."

"But I thought you two were..." Heather didn't know how to say what they were, because she didn't know, so she just shrugged.

Ashley didn't seem to care. "Even though your aunt told me he was a womanizer, I'm not ready to give up on him yet. I know I can change him."

"If you think so." *This girl must be delusional.* Heather had tried the same thing with Jack. Only to be disappointed. "So what's your favor? You know I'd do anything to help."

Ashley's large, fawn-colored eyes misted. "Please have dinner at the Vendeglo restaurant this evening, and let me know if Miklos is entertaining his ex-girlfriend there. Maybe your aunt could go with you."

Heather shook her head. "Anything but that."

Ashley offered a weak smile. "You don't have to pay. It would be my treat."

"It's not the money. My aunt is eating dinner at the retirement village today and playing cards afterwards. Even though I don't like eating alone, I'd do it for you. But not at the Vendeglo."

"Don't you like their food?"

"I love Hungarian food. It's Miklos's brother Sandos I can't stand. Every time I go in there, that tattooed, love-struck body-builder makes a pass at me and insists he sit at my table, where he talks about everything we *don't* have in common. I've staved him off so far, but if I keep going to his restaurant, especially alone, he'll think I'm interested."

Ashley put her hands over her face and sobbed. "You were my only hope."

"Don't you have any other friends you can ask?"

"All of my close female friends have moved out of town, and the friends I have left here are fair-weather at best. I can't trust them, anyway. They're all after Miklos."

"Maybe there's something else we can think of," Heather said. "But honestly, I don't know why you're trying so hard. I tried to change Jack Steele's womanizing ways. It didn't work. Is he really worth your time and your tears?"

"This is different. Miklos is different." A moment later, Ashley perked up. "I know it didn't work for you, but maybe it'll work for me. There was something your aunt told me last night. She said jealousy is a two-way street. I know if Miklos sees me with another man, he'll get jealous, and he'll want me back."

"Then, why don't *you* go to dinner at the Vendeglo? All you need is a handsome escort. What about that guy who was in here a couple of weeks ago? You know, the one who helped me with my aunt's digital camera?"

"Kyle Edwards? No. Miklos knows Kyle from high school. He'd never be jealous of him. Besides, Kyle has a girlfriend."

Heather rubbed her forehead trying to come up with another way. "So we just have to find someone else in Willows Bend. Someone tall, good-looking, and sophisticated."

"Like Jack?"

Heather's eyes bugged out. "Steele?" She put a hand to her throat. "That's a terrible idea."

She didn't want to get involved with Jack again. Besides, Chad didn't like Miklos, and if she helped Ashley win him back, he might never speak to her again.

"It's okay." Ashley's eyes misted, and she offered Heather a broken smile. "You don't have to ask him. I'll find someone else."

Heather thought about it for a few minutes. It pained her to see her friend this way. She hated to ask Jack anything, but for Ashley, she might have to make an exception. Then an idea struck her.

"Maybe I won't have to ask Jack. If I can get him to come to the bookstore, do you think you could convince him to go out to dinner with you?"

"I can try," Ashley said. "But I can't think of a reason why he'd want to."

"Leave it to me." Heather grabbed her cell phone, and as chance would have it, she remembered Jack's cell number.

He picked up on the first ring. "Well, hello. What a surprise to hear from you."

"Don't get your hopes up. I just need you to settle an argument." She winked at Ashley. "Do you remember that Hungarian restaurant we used to frequent in Chicago?"

"Yeah, why?"

"I'm at the *Willow in the Wind* bookstore having a little disagreement with the owner about Hungarian food. You remember her—the beautiful brunette behind the front counter?"

After a moment's hesitation, he said, "I'll be right over."

Heather knew the words, "beautiful brunette" would get to him. She couldn't help but smile at Ashley. "He's on his way, and he's all yours. Tell him I had an appointment, so I had to leave, and then get into a disagreement about some particular Hungarian food. Pick anything. Jack loves to argue food... thinks he's a connoisseur. After he gives you his opinion, which may take a while, invite him to dinner at the Vendeglo tonight to prove *your* point."

Ashley's grin was the best thanks Heather could get. She just hoped Jack could make Miklos jealous. Who was she kidding? Jack could make any man jealous.

"Before you leave," Ashley said, "There's one person who might be a slight problem."

Heather nodded. "I know. Your brother. He won't be happy that you're out with Jack."

Ashley smirked. "He might not like it, but he won't stop me. I can date whoever I want." She pressed her lips together in thought. "But there's a way to *distract* my brother, if you'll help."

"How can I refuse? Just don't ever let him find out I was your accomplice."

Chapter 19

BACK in her apartment, Heather rummaged through the kitchen cabinets looking for something she could serve Chad for dinner. She pulled out a jar of peanut butter, two tins of sardines, and a box of crackers. *Is this all we have?* The only things in the refrigerator were a few half-empty condiment jars and last night's leftovers from Christine's. *That would be great to serve, except he also ate that for dinner last night.* She'd never pass it off as her own. And besides, he probably had a refrigerator full of it too.

The freezer was her last hope. She grabbed a bag of frozen shrimp. *Garlic Shrimp and Pasta* was her quick, go-to meal when she couldn't find anything else to eat.

And she'd even picked up Chad's favorite dessert on the way to the police station earlier, dark chocolate fudge with walnuts. She'd drop a glop of vanilla ice cream on top of a large chunk. Vanilla ice cream was something she always kept on hand. It went with just about every dessert or even as dessert by itself. *That should put him in a good mood. I might even get a goodnight kiss this time. Unless Aunt Julia gets home early. Better not get my hopes up.*

She checked the clock on the stove. Time to call Chad. She tapped his name on her contact list.

He answered on the second ring. "Hey. I was just thinking about you."

"I wanted to thank you again for dinner the other night. Since my aunt will be out all evening, I'd like to make you dinner at my apartment tonight. Are you free?"

"Just me?"

"Just you."

"Sure. What time?"

Ashley was asking Jack to pick her up at seven, so…

"Around six-thirty?" She crossed her fingers.

"I'll be there."

"See you then." She ended the call and breathed a sigh of relief. *So far, so good. Except for one small oversight.*

Heather tapped Ashley's number.

"I can't invite Chad to dinner tonight. I don't have a table or chairs. My aunt and I have been eating off of the kitchen counter, but I can't put candles on a kitchen counter and expect it to look romantic."

Ashley giggled. "My brother can be such a dope sometimes. Didn't he tell you about the folding table and chairs in the laundry room? Granddad used to hold poker games on Saturday nights with some of his unsavory friends."

"No, Chad never said anything."

"The table is shoved between the washer and the dryer. And there are two folding chairs hanging on the back of the door, but I can't remember where the other chairs are. They might be in one of the bedroom closets or up in the attic."

"That's okay. I only need two chairs. Thanks, Ash."

Heather ended the call and dashed for the laundry room.

<><><>

After spreading her large, burgundy silk wrap as a table cloth, she lit the black candles leftover from one of Aunt Julia's scary rituals and set the silverware at each place setting.

Then she made the garlic sauce and put the frozen shrimp in the frying pan while the pasta boiled. She set a timer and went to finish her hair.

A knock at the front door had her checking her cell phone for the time. "He's early. It's only a little past six."

She didn't have time to blow her hair out properly, so she shook it out, letting the loose curls fall where they may, and answered the door.

Jack Steele stormed into her apartment. "You tricked me."

I don't have time for this. "What are you talking about?"

"That beautiful brunette you told me about in the bookstore is in a wheelchair!"

"So. What difference does *that* make? She's still beautiful."

"Yes, but she's in a wheelchair."

"Jack Steele, you're a bigot."

"I am not. It's just that she's..."

"Don't say it again." Heather put her hand up to stop him. "Listen Jack, you'd better go out to dinner with that woman, or I'll tell all your friends you're a bigot!"

His face turned a light shade of pink. "Okay, I'll do it, but only to prove the point that the Hungarian food here isn't half as good as it is in Chicago."

Heather smiled, pleased with herself. "I've tasted it. You'll be surprised. It's better." She pushed him toward the door. "Now, please go. I'm expecting a guest for dinner."

Jack gave the room a quick once over. "Candles... romantic." And then he pointed to her head. "I hate your hair that way."

She glared at him, counting the seconds until he was out of her sight. "I don't care what you hate. That lovely woman downstairs is waiting for you to pick her up for dinner, so go!"

She swung the door open for him to leave. And came face to face with Jimmy the Horse.

"Hi Jimmy," Jack said as the older man stormed into the apartment.

"Julie!" Jimmy called out.

Oh no! What now?

Jimmy ducked his head into each room. "Where is she?"

The knot in Heather's stomach tightened. "As you can see, she's not home. And she may not be for days. So you might as well leave."

She glared at Jack as he stood near the door. "Don't you have somewhere to be?"

Jimmy eyed her from head to toe and back again. "Then what are you doing here?"

"I'm making dinner," was all she could think of to say.

"Why are you making dinner *here* if you live upstairs?"

"If you must know, I'm just using her kitchen. So, if that's all, please leave."

Jimmy handed Heather his card. "Call me when Julie comes home."

As if that's gonna happen.

She nodded anyway. "I will. Now, please go."

He went out the door, passing Jack who was standing on the landing outside the door, texting.

"Why are you still here?" Heather asked.

He leaned on the door frame. "Don't rush me."

The oven timer shrieked from the other room. Beads of perspiration formed at Heather's hairline. She ran to the kitchen and turned it off along with the burner under her pasta. She put a strainer in the sink and dumped the contents of the pot into it. The now partially defrosted shrimp lying in the frying pan looked positively pathetic, but she was glad she'd made the garlic sauce earlier. Now all she had to do was put everything together. But first...

Heather rushed back into the living room. Jack stood on the top step, still texting.

"I told you to leave." She slammed the door shut, but a few moments later it was opened by her aunt who rushed into the apartment.

My head is going to explode. "What are you doing home so early? What happened to your card game?"

"Detective Lindsey broke it up, and then he grilled me because the police received an anonymous tip that I was spotted near the crime scene around the time the murder took place. And I have a good idea who made that call."

Heather gave her a crooked smile, halfway between a frown and a grin. *I don't believe this.*

Julia's eyes blazed. "And if he thinks he's going to frame me for Denny's murder, Jimmy's got another thing coming." She turned to close the door. "Oh, hi, Jack. What are you doing here?"

A huge grin spread across Jack's handsome face. "Sounds like you might need a criminal lawyer." He pulled several business cards from his wallet and sifted through them. Then he pulled one out and handed it to her. "I have a friend who's a shark. He's in high demand, but tell him I sent you, and he'll take you on."

You mean he's a shyster. Heather had about enough of Jack for one evening. She hated confrontations, but this one was necessary. "Jack, I asked you to go. Now get *Out!*"

He turned and stomped down the stairs. Heather closed her eyes and breathed a sigh of relief.

When she opened them again, Chad was standing at the door, glancing over his shoulder at Jack retreating down the stairs. Her heart dropped to the floor. This is not how she imagined the evening would begin.

"If I'd known it was going to be a party," he said, "I would've brought more wine." He held out a bottle of Champagne. "I didn't know what we were having for dinner, so I thought I'd be safe, because you know..." He winked. "It goes with everything."

How sweet. He remembered. Heather raised her arms and dropped them at her sides in frustration. "It's perfect. Thank you. I'll put it in the fridge for now."

Chad's brow scrunched as he pointed toward the door. "What was Jack doing here? I thought you said you were through with him for good."

Chapter 20

HEATHER wiped the perspiration from her forehead. "I am. He just came to leave a friend's business card for my aunt, in case she needs a criminal lawyer."

Julia sucked in a breath and murmured something to herself as she let it out. Heather had no interest in what she was saying. All she wanted was for her aunt to leave, but it didn't look like that was going to happen any time soon.

Julia blew out the candles on the table. "You should never light black candles unless you're going to do an occult ritual. Otherwise, you're attracting serious bad luck."

At this point, Heather wanted to cry. "I found *that* out the hard way."

"Where did you get the card table and chairs?" Then Julia's mouth dropped open as if a realization had just dawned on her. She slapped her cheek. "Oh, I'm sorry."

She scurried toward the kitchen. "Never mind. I'll ask you about it later. You two go ahead with your romantic dinner. Don't mind me. I'll just take a cup of coffee and grab one of these chocolate walnut fudge bars for a snack. Then I'll go to my room. You won't even know I'm here."

Heather couldn't help but frown. "Famous last words."

Chad stood in the kitchen doorway with his arms folded across his muscular chest. "Somehow, knowing your aunt will be in the next room just took the romance right out of dinner for me."

"Me too," Heather agreed. "But at least we can eat."

After dinner, Heather poured the coffee and set dessert on the table. Chad finished his before she did. He sat back in his chair and crossed his legs. "I really enjoyed that. You're a wonderful cook."

"Thank you. I'm so glad you liked it." Heather didn't want to admit shrimp in garlic sauce was the only meal she was any good at making. Instead, she excused herself from the table to send Ashley a text asking when she'd be home.

She walked into her bedroom and glanced in the mirror. At first, the shock made her stare at her reflection. Strands of hair stuck out, and curls hung in awkward directions. "Oh my God! With everything that happened, I forgot to comb my hair."

She laughed in embarrassment. Had she looked this hideous all evening? Why didn't anyone say anything? Well, except Jack. She should have listened and gone back to the bathroom to fix it.

She grabbed a brush and finally got it looking the way she intended it to look. Then she texted Ashley.

The answer was, "Not soon enough for me."

That doesn't sound good. She started to text back to ask her what happened, but the sound of voices emanating from the living room drew her in that direction.

Aunt Julia sat at the table across from Chad. She turned her head when Heather came into the room. "I noticed you were finished eating, so I came out to ask Chad for a favor. I hope that's okay with you."

What happened to, "You won't even know I'm here?"

"It's not my call to make," Heather said.

Chad glanced at Heather before returning his attention to Julia. "I'll be glad to help you any way I can."

"Feel free to refuse." Heather pressed her lips together and glared at her aunt.

"Like I was saying," Julia continued. "It appears that Jimmy is trying to make it look like I killed Denny Serrano. And I realize you're not a private investigator anymore. But in order for me to turn the tables on him, I need to find out a few things, like what he's doing for a living these days. He says he's in business, but what kind of business? Also, what kind of relationship did he have with Denny?"

Julia wagged a finger for emphasis. "I have a feeling there's more to that relationship than meets the eye. I can think of a couple of reasons why Jimmy might want Denny dead, like witnessing a murder Jimmy committed. Or if Denny stole money from Jimmy's 'business' —which is conning people. And not nice people either, ruthless people who are probably demanding payback. That could also be why he's trying to get money from me now... to cover his losses."

"But why would Jimmy kill a man who owed him money?" Heather asked.

"I'll find out what I can. What's Jimmy the Horse's last name?"

"Marlucci." Julia spelled it for him.

"Oh, by the way," Heather suddenly remembered. "Jimmy was here looking for you earlier this evening."

"What did he want?" Julia asked.

"I don't know, but he was in a bad mood and extremely insistent on seeing you."

"If either of you come across him again, just say you don't know where I am. I'm going to try to evade him as long as possible, or at least until I can figure out what he's up to."

Chad stood. "I'll do my best. But I can't guarantee I'll find out anything that might be useful to you."

"Whatever you discover that can be used in my favor is fine," Julia said. "And I'll see if any of my old contacts are willing to spill what they know about those two guys. Jimmy wasn't well-liked in the old days. The man conned pretty much everyone he's ever met."

Heather thought of more questions, but she didn't want to get her aunt wound up for the evening, or she'd end up talking for hours. She silently cleared the table and set the dishes in the sink. Her questions could wait until tomorrow.

This was not the evening Heather had planned. Her hopes for a goodnight kiss were dwindling as the evening wore on. She walked back into the living room to see if she missed collecting anything, but Julia had already pulled the shawl off the table and spread it over the back of the sofa. She was now struggling to fold the table legs.

Chad eased the table from her grip. "There's a trick to that."

He showed Julia the easy way to get the legs folded under. Then he took the table to the laundry room. Heather followed him, carrying the folding chairs.

"Thanks for doing that." She handed him the chairs to hang behind the door.

"It's the least I could do. I'm sorry I forgot to tell you about these. But you're very clever to have discovered them on your own."

"Actually, your sister told me." Heather put her hands on her hips. "Is there anything else I'll eventually discover in this apartment that you've forgotten to tell me about?"

Chad gave her a sly smile. "One never knows what one might find in this apartment. I've noticed it's smaller than the store downstairs. Makes me wonder if there aren't some hiding places up here."

Then he walked out of the laundry room, leaving Heather to wonder too. She followed him toward the back door.

He opened it and turned to face her. "I'm assuming dinner is over."

Julia was pouring herself another cup of decaf in the kitchen and humming to herself. Chad stepped out the back door onto the landing, guiding Heather out along with him. He closed the door, his eyes flashing as he stared at her. The warm evening breeze caressed her face, and her heart raced in anticipation.

Heather lifted her chin. "I don't want you to think I invited you to dinner so my aunt could ask you for help. She told me she was going out for the evening."

"The best laid plans?"

"Something like that."

He put his arms around her. "The best laid plans sometimes turn out better than expected." His lips lightly touched hers, and then he deepened the kiss. With her heart on fire, she couldn't help returning his passion.

The back door opened. Chad broke the kiss, taking his arms from around Heather, as if he was caught doing something he shouldn't.

"Oh, I'm sorry," Julia said. "I thought Chad had already gone. You two go back to doing what you were doing."

Chad checked his cell phone. "It's getting late. I really have to go. Thanks for the delicious dinner, Heather." He turned and rushed down the back stairs to his car. Fortunately, the police had finally taken the crime scene tape down.

"You're welcome," Heather called after him. She dropped her shoulders and went inside, slamming the back door behind her.

"Really, Aunt Julia!"

Chapter 21

WEDNESDAY morning at City Hall dragged on as Heather searched website after website, comparing prices on products and services for the dance hall so she could fit them into her budget."

She closed her dry eyes for a moment to rest them and daydreamed about last night's kiss and where it might have led if they hadn't been interrupted. After a few moments, Heather tried to go back to work, but she couldn't get that image out of her head.

A rapid knock on the door startled her, and she jumped out of her chair to answer it. No one ever came to her office, unless they were interested in using it to store something.

The mayor's administrative assistant stuck her head inside. "I'm taking orders from the deli for lunch and wondered if you'd like anything."

Heather checked her wall clock. Ten after twelve. She glanced at her empty coffee cup. Her growling stomach reminded her she needed to eat. Food might also help to get rid of the brain fog slowly setting in.

Sylvia handed Heather a page with *Manny's Deli Take-out Menu* printed on it.

Heather scanned it. "I thought the mayor always ate at The Athena."

"He does. This is for some of the office workers in the building who can't afford to eat there every day."

Heather had to ask. "Does the mayor's accountant eat at The Athena too?"

Sylvia scrunched her eyes in a look of suspicion. "Why do you ask?"

"No reason." Heather tried to sound uninterested as she checked the prices on everything from the soup of the day to dozens of delicious-sounding deli sandwiches, desserts, and drinks.

"Everything looks great. But I have a refrigerator full of leftovers at home I have to eat before they go bad. Thanks for thinking of me."

Sylvia shrugged and took the menu back. "In answer to your question, where the mayor goes, his accountant goes," she said with a note of sarcasm. "They've been working on some special project the mayor wants completed by the end of his term, and a tight financial picture must be a part of it. Of course, I'm just guessing. I haven't been privy to what they're doing, which makes me suspicious. But it is what it is." The disdain in her voice was unmistakable. Sylvia was clearly not happy about not being included in whatever the secret was between the two men.

After the second day of being leftover in the refrigerator, Christine's lasagna still tasted delicious, even microwaved. There was no garlic bread, so Heather toasted a piece of white bread, slathered butter on it, and sprinkled the top with garlic powder. *Not exactly the same but edible*. After she'd eaten, she set the dishes in the sink and grabbed a cold Pepsi from the fridge on her way out the back door.

She pulled the knob until she heard a solid click to make sure it was locked. With all the dreadful events going on since Jimmy the Horse came to town, she didn't want to take any chances.

It was evident Jimmy wanted something from Julia, but she wouldn't give an inch. Could she still have $200,000 stashed away somewhere? No. She'd explained what happened to *that* money. But there were days when Heather couldn't help but wonder.

As Heather traipsed down the stairs, Ashley Willows, in her white dress pants and pink print top, sat in her wheelchair by Heather's rental car. "I thought I heard you come home for lunch."

"Hi Ash. How did your date with Jack go?"

Ashley dragged her hands over her pale face.

"It was brutal." She crooked a finger, signaling Heather to come closer. "I don't want Chad to hear."

Ashley rolled her chair around the building until she was on the sidewalk next to it.

Heather followed. "Your dinner couldn't have been worse than mine." She grimaced. "First, Jack showed up. Then Jimmy the Horse arrived. I'd just gotten Jimmy to go when my aunt came home. And *then* your brother arrived. I finally got Jack to leave but not my aunt. I never got the chance to comb my hair, so it was sticking out in every direction all through dinner, although your brother kindly never mentioned it. When I finally realized it was a mess and got the chance to fix it, I walked back into the living room as my aunt was in the middle of asking your brother for a favor. It looked like I invited him to dinner so she could put him on the spot for help."

"That was pretty bad," Ashley said. "But mine was worse."

Heather leaned against the building and crossed her arms as she listened.

"First of all, Jack texted me he'd be late picking me up. So he was at your place all that time?"

"Yes, I'm sorry to say he was."

"He did finally pick me up, but when we got to the restaurant, an hour after our reservation, who do we run into waiting to be seated but Krystal Stamos? I had this gut feeling the whole thing was pre-arranged by Jack. Anyway, it was bad enough she invited us to sit at her table, but she and Jack were all over each other during dinner, and I had to spend the evening dealing with not only *your* ex-boyfriend but my brother's ex- fiancée."

Heather couldn't think of anything worse. "That really *was* brutal."

"Then Sandos stopped at our table to welcome us to the restaurant. I couldn't help but ask if Miklos was there. He said his brother was away on personal business that evening, but he'd tell him I asked about him. I was mortified."

She put her hands over her face again. "I *am* mortified. Why couldn't I keep my big mouth shut?"

"You'll just have to wait it out," Heather said. "If Miklos wants to call you, he will. If you don't hear from him, there's not much you can do and still keep your dignity."

"You're right." Ashley took her hands down. "I've been crying for the past two days and nights. I don't think I have any more tears left in me."

She sighed and glanced at her cell phone. "I have to get back inside. Chad's looking for me."

Heather grabbed the handle on the back door to open it for Ashley and saw Chad standing there. Her heart flipped. “I’d better get back to work,” she stammered, hoping he hadn’t overheard their conversation.

Chapter 22

AFTER an afternoon of trying to put together a budget the mayor would accept, Heather was glad to be home again. But before she could relax, she had to check the back door. Everything appeared secure, so she chucked off her white flats and slipped into a pair of comfortable house slippers. Then she grabbed a few tea bags and boiled some water for iced tea. *Aunt Julia will appreciate this.*

She had just set the finished pitcher in the refrigerator when the front door opened, and Julia sauntered into the living room.

She kicked off her shoes and plopped down on the sofa. "What a day I've had."

Heather put a tall glass of iced tea in her hand.

"Thanks. I could use this." She gulped down half a glass and set it on a coaster on the coffee table.

Heather picked up her glass and sat on one of the overstuffed wing chairs opposite the fireplace. "Did you find out anything about Jimmy the Horse?"

"On my lunch hour, I called two of my old contacts in Chicago. Unfortunately, they're both in prison at the moment—so no help there. Then I seemed to recall there was a wife somewhere in Denny Serrano's past.

She might have been related to Jimmy. I've been trying to remember her first name and where she lived all afternoon."

Heather pulled out her laptop. "Let's see what we can find about her online."

"It's very sweet of you to offer, but I don't remember where they were married or if they were divorced. And I doubt if any of them have a Facebook page or a Twitter account."

"A marriage and a divorce are matters of public record. There might be something out there. I'll check anyway."

After a half hour of searching, Heather came up with nothing. "There must be something about them somewhere. There has to be a marriage license on record, and they have to have relatives."

Heather checked the time on her laptop. It was five-thirty, and the bookstore closed at six on Wednesdays. She rushed to the front door. "I have to go downstairs and talk to Chad about something."

"Can't you phone him?"

"No. It's not something I can talk to him about on the phone."

"Wait," Julia said. "I'll go with you. I want to find out what he uncovered today."

Heather slipped back into her shoes, grabbed her keys and locked the door behind them. She didn't want to take the chance of finding Jimmy in there when they returned.

The heavy oak door of the old bookstore opened with a slight creak and a loud jingle, alerting everyone inside that potential customers had walked in.

Ashley, seated in her usual spot behind the counter, put her cell phone down and greeted them. "Hi ladies. What's up?"

Makki sauntered up to Heather's feet and meowed. She stooped down to pet his soft fur, and he raised his back to meet her hand. She stayed down as Makki rubbed his face against her leg.

"I wish I had a treat to give you," Heather said. "But I'll remember to bring one next time."

Her aunt looked at them. "He doesn't understand a thing you're saying."

"I wouldn't be so sure." Heather stood, still gazing at Makki. "He's a pretty smart cat."

Julia turned to Chad who's smile warmed Heather's heart. He evidently hadn't heard anything she and Ashley discussed at lunchtime.

"Have you found out anything today?" Julia asked him.

He led them to his laptop on a table in the back room and pressed a few keys as he sat in front of it.

"Jimmy's been arrested several times on petty charges, but he hasn't been convicted of anything major since you turned him in to the Feds. He and Denny were partners in a Ponzi Scheme that took a nosedive when Denny overplayed his part. Now Jimmy owes big money to a mob boss."

Julia rubbed her chin. "I knew it had to be something like that. He really does need the $200,000. And probably a lot more. What else do you have?"

Chad scrunched his eyes. "Wait a minute. What $200,000?"

"The money I took with me when I left Vegas after I turned him in to the Feds."

Heather wasn't so sure the money was what Jimmy wanted from her aunt. She had a feeling it was something else.

Chad shook his head. "Well, that clears things up." He scrolled down the screen. "There's more. Denny married Jimmy's only sister, Joan, when Jimmy was in prison. Denny got her hooked on drugs. She did several stints in rehab to kick the habit and is currently doing another, but she's not in the best of health."

"That sounds like two motives to kill Denny," Julia said.

As Ashley rolled into the room, Heather looked at her aunt. "I have to agree with you about the motives."

Julia scrunched her eyes. "You know what this means, don't you?"

As usual, Heather had no idea.

Julia then raised her index finger in the air for emphasis. "It's time to go to the mattresses."

Both Chad and Ashley burst out laughing.

"You sound like the Godfather," Chad said.

Julia wasn't laughing. "The idea is to get Jimmy to confess." She paced the room. "I think I know where I might be able to get a horse's head."

Heather rolled her eyes. This situation was getting ridiculous. "Aunt Julia, you're not a mobster in a movie."

Julia gave her a sideways glance. "We'll see. Christine is working at the Franklin House tonight. She always works the front desk on the night shift when George is on the road because she thinks her house is haunted." Julia waved her hand. "But that's another story. Anyway, she can let me know when Jimmy's out and then let me into his room."

"Christine may not be so easy to convince," Heather said. "She could lose her job if anyone finds out she gave you his room key."

"Not if the cards say it's okay."

I see she's thought of everything. "But I doubt Jimmy will confess to murder if he wants his sister to be able to collect Denny's insurance money."

"Why?" Julia said. "She didn't kill him, so she can still collect the insurance." She put a finger to her lips. "Hmmm. I can search his room for a clue. I remember he liked to hide things under his mattress. Doesn't trust hotel safes."

"But you won't be able to use anything you find there against him." Ashley chimed in. "And what if he's not guilty. We still have to find out who killed Denny Serrano."

Chapter 23

"WE?" Chad said. "How did you and I get involved in solving this murder?"

Ashley opened her eyes wide like a doe caught in a headlight. "It happened right outside our back door. How can we ignore that? It's practically our duty to at least help find out 'who done it'."

"And I need all the help I can get," Julia said.

Chad wrinkled his brow. "I think this is better left to Detective Lindsey to solve. That's his job. But I have to admit, it appears as if there was no one else in town who had a motive to kill Denny Serrano except Jimmy the Horse."

"How do you know that?" Heather asked. "According to Christine Talan, Denny was here for over a week before Jimmy arrived. He may have pulled a scam on someone to make a few bucks."

"Yeah," Julia said. "That would be just like him. And probably on someone who couldn't afford to lose the money. He loved to prey on the vulnerable. And if I remember how Denny operated, it was probably much more than a few dollars. Maybe even someone's life savings. But we'd have to get access to his bank account to prove it. And I don't think there's any way we can do that. Is there?" Julia's brown eyes bulged as she stared expectantly at Chad.

He turned his head toward the wall, refusing to acknowledge the question.

"Chad, Officer Henderson is your friend," Ashley said. "Can't he find out for us?"

Chad opened his mouth and then closed it, letting out a heavy sigh. "I'm sure if someone was swindled out of his or her life savings, they would have reported it to the police."

"Not if the person was too ashamed to admit it," Julia said. "If your friend won't give you the information, can he at least get me into the evidence room at the police station so I can see if there's something of Denny's that could be a clue to his murder? Something Lindsey might not consider important?"

Chad shook his head. "I can't ask any of my friends to put their job on the line like that. Not to mention the fact that if anyone found out we broke the chain of evidence, any evidence you *did* manage to find would be rendered inadmissible."

The bell on the front door jingled. Ashley checked her cell.

"I knew I should have locked the door. It's after six o'clock. We're supposed to be closed." She wheeled herself back into the bookstore.

Following his sister, Chad glanced over his shoulder. His eyes met Heather's, and her heart melted under his gaze.

"There's something I want to talk to *you* about," he said.

She didn't like the way he emphasized the word *you*. Sounded accusatory. *I hope he hasn't found out about the fix-up with his sister and Jack Steele.* Her scalp tingled, and her palms began to sweat, the way they always did when she hoped something wasn't true but knew the truth would surface eventually.

Detective Lindsey sauntered into the back room. "Miss Stanton. I thought I might find you here, since you didn't answer your door upstairs."

A mild heat rose to Heather's cheeks. "What can I do for you, Detective?"

"You said you were coming to the station after work today, but you never showed up."

"I was there." Her shoulders rose defensively. "But I saw you come out of the building, get in your car, and drive away. So I went home. I was planning to come back tomorrow."

Lindsey nodded. "That must have been right after I got the anonymous tip about your aunt."

Julia came up to the detective and stuck her nose in his face. "And then you broke up my pinochle game."

"That was no pinochle game. That's why I broke it up. Money was on the table, and the game you were playing was Five Card Stud."

"I can explain what you think you saw. The reason there was money on the table was because Eloise wanted change for a ten dollar bill, so I threw the change on the table, but before I could pick up the ten, you came in and broke up the game. Playing poker for money is illegal in Illinois."

"Sorry, Julia." The detective eyed her with suspicion. "I know what I saw. Don't try to gaslight me, because it won't work."

"Well, after that, at least you've eliminated me as a suspect."

"Not quite. You don't have an alibi for the time of the murder, and you've admitted you knew the victim, one of only two people in town who did. So let's just say you're still a person of interest."

Julia batted her eyelashes at him. "I always knew you were interested in me."

"It's not that kind of interest." The detective's voice sounded serious.

Julia huffed and crossed her arms. "Well, if you're going to take that stance, you're forgetting one thing. I also don't have a motive."

"I'm working on that."

Julia swung around, turning her back to him.

"It seems to me, Detective," Heather tried to bring the voice of reason to this insane conversation. "There was only one man who had a motive, actually two motives, to murder Denny Serrano, and that was his boss, Jimmy the Horse."

"How do you know Jimmy was his boss?"

"Because he admitted he sent Denny here to find my aunt. Did you question Jimmy yet?"

"Of course I did."

Julia swung around. "Do you know Jimmy has a record?"

"I do, and I know all about your connection."

Julia sniffed. "So what did he say about me?"

The detective opened his mouth and raised his eyebrows. "Hey, I'm asking the questions here."

"May I suggest you let my aunt look at the evidence you have, since she knew the victim? Maybe she can see something you didn't know was a clue."

Detective Lindsey gazed at Julia a moment. Then his gaze went back to Heather. "No, I can't let a suspect... I mean a person of interest, examine the evidence. But," he pointed at Julia, "I can go over it again myself if you'll tell me what I should be looking for."

Chad walked in. "We have to close the store. Are you finished in here, Detective?"

"No, but you can close," Lindsey said. "We'll continue our discussion at the station. I still need to get a statement from you, Heather, so why don't you and Julia follow me there."

"Sure," Heather agreed.

At least she'd have her aunt for support, and she wasn't looking forward to being given a lecture from Chad about how disappointed he was in her for setting his sister up on a date with Jack Steele.

Chapter 24

After Heather gave her statement to Detective Lindsey, her aunt joined them at his desk.

Julia tried to talk him into letting her see the evidence. "It's not always what's there," she explained. "Sometimes it's what's not there that can be a clue."

He sat shaking his head with a blank expression on his face.

An officer Heather had never seen before placed a file folder on his desk. "Something just came up."

"Later," Lindsey said to him.

"It's important."

"All right." Lindsey opened the folder. After reading what it said, he closed it. "Well, this changes things."

Heather exchanged glances with her aunt.

Julia shrugged. "What's that? Did you find out some new information about the case?"

Lindsey tapped his fingers on the desk in a gesture of frustration. "It appears that Denny was poisoned."

"Poisoned?" Julia asked. "With what?"

"According to the report, there were several different poisons in his system when he died. Belladonna, atropine, and traces of scopolamine."

"That's an odd mixture," Heather said.

Julia's eyes widened. "Sounds like the ingredients in one of Madam Z's special elixirs." A few moments later, she leaned forward. "As a matter of fact, Madam Z had a garden behind her studio with all kinds of flowers and herbs. They were lovely to look at, but many of them were deadly if you ingested them."

Detective Lindsey searched his computer and typed something into it. A few moments later he slapped his desk. "You're right, Julia. All three of these toxins are found in one plant—Atropa Belladonna."

"Of course, Deadly Nightshade," Julia said. "Madame Z grew it in what she liked to call, her *garden of earthy delights*."

Heather bit her bottom lip. "But how does someone extract poison from a plant?"

"Anyone can do it," Julia said. "The internet is full of information on how to do things. And then of course, Madam Z sold all kinds of custom-made elixirs. That could have been an ingredient in one of them."

"She also never kept any records," Lindsay said.

Julia waved a finger at the detective. "Denny could have unknowingly eaten or drunk something with the poison in it. The effects might not have fully kicked in until he reached the top landing of our back stairs. I bet he started feeling sick or dizzy, and he passed out and fell down the staircase, breaking his neck when he hit the pavement at the bottom." Her eyes sparkled. "I solved the case!"

"Wait a minute," Lindsey said. "Not so fast. We still have to find out how he was poisoned, where he was poisoned, and who did it." He put his hands on his knees and stood. "How do I know it wasn't you who invited him in for breakfast on Sunday morning, dumped poison into his scrambled eggs or coffee, and then pushed him down the stairs?"

Julia's eyes narrowed. "Because he didn't have breakfast with me on Sunday. I didn't even know he was in town. Haven't you questioned the folks at the retirement village yet."

"No. We haven't gotten around to questioning anyone there. But you evidently have. Why?"

"Because," Julia put her hands out, "three of the residents were having breakfast at The Athena on Sunday morning and saw him there with Jimmy the Horse, Johnny Tanner, and the mayor's assistant, Sylvia. We know Jimmy had more than one solid motive to kill Denny."

The detective leaned toward her. "Where would Jimmy get his hands on the poison plant? He didn't know Madam Z."

Julia shook her head. "Maybe he bought it from someone in town."

"Seems unlikely." Lindsey turned to Heather. "You were at the restaurant Sunday morning. Did you see them?"

"No, but I didn't get there until eleven. They were probably gone by then. I did see the mayor and his accountant."

Lindsey's eyes narrowed. "Maybe it's time I had a talk with the people at the retirement village." He turned to Julia and opened his notebook. "I need names."

<><><>

As they walked side-by-side back to Heather's rental car in the parking lot, Julia said, "I hope I haven't cast suspicion on my friends at the retirement village. As it is, they'll probably never ask me to play cards with them again."

Heather pulled her keys out of her purse. "I'm sure they understand this is a murder investigation, and questioning is just routine. Who knows, they may have something enlightening to tell Lindsey. But what surprised me was how cooperative *you* were. You're usually so belligerent."

"Yeah, well—situations change. You know the old saying, 'You can catch more flies with honey.' I thought I'd try a different strategy this time. Did you see the look on his face when I actually answered his questions without giving him a hard time? Priceless! Besides, I'm tired of sitting at home on Saturday nights, and there aren't any other good-looking, eligible men around my age in this town. At least, none that I've met yet."

They got into the car, and Heather turned on the engine. Her dashboard clock read 6:47 p.m. "I didn't realize it was so late. But I don't feel like eating sardines for dinner. Got any suggestions?"

"While we're here," Julia said, "Why don't you stop at the Club Car Diner around the corner and pick up a couple of Polish sausage sandwiches and some fries?"

Heather's mouth watered at the thought of the delicious, spicy sandwich as she pulled her car out of the lot, but she was broke. "Sorry, I don't have any extra money right now."

"My treat," Julia said. "I got lucky playing the horses today. I didn't win a lot but enough to buy us a couple of sausage sandwiches. Looks like I'm making some progress toward that evil curse being broken."

"Great," Heather said. "I'm glad to hear it, because I'm starving."

She pulled her car up in front of the glorified hot dog stand with its Kelly green and white striped awning and turned off the engine.

Julia handed her some money and got out of the car. "It's such a beautiful day. I thought we could eat outdoors for a change. I'll grab us an empty picnic table around the back, and you buy the sandwiches and a couple of colas."

"Sounds good to me," Heather said.

With the temperature in the upper 70s, the mild evening breeze carried the spicy scents emanating from the hot dog stand mixed with the light smell of fresh cut grass, not at all like the stifling stench of car fumes in downtown Chicago she was used to. She took in a deep breath and enjoyed the clear air as she sauntered up to the counter and placed her order. After a few moments, she headed around the back, two white paper bags in hand.

As she turned the corner, Julia waved to her from one of the six redwood picnic tables that were set on a square slab of concrete behind the hot dog stand. She was not alone.

Heather made her way to the table and set the bags down. She smiled her hello and sat next to her aunt.

"Look who I found sitting back here, eating dinner," Julia said.

Chad nodded as he chewed a mouthful of burger. His friend Sam, a.k.a. Officer Henderson, wearing street clothes, sat across from him munching on a hot dog with everything on it.

"I thought you'd be eating dinner with your sister," Heather said to Chad.

He swallowed and wiped his mouth with a napkin. "I just dropped her off at the day spa. She's having an exercise session. Then she's going to the hair salon. She'll be gone for hours."

Heather wished she had the kind of money she used to spend at that fabulous hair salon in Chicago where she'd had a standing appointment every Thursday evening. It was the one thing she missed about not working downtown.

"Thought I'd grab a burger on my way home," Chad continued. "And I ran into Sam."

Someone had once told her the police ate here a lot, being in such close proximity to the station house.

Sam's lips curved into friendly smile. "Nice to see you again, Heather. We've just been talking to your aunt."

She was surprised the officer even acknowledged her aunt, and with such a pleasant greeting. After all the hard times Julia had given him in the past, she thought he'd be irritated to see her. But as she'd discovered over the last few weeks about the tall, muscular officer with the chestnut-colored hair and pleasant features, he had an extremely tolerant nature.

"Your aunt said Detective Lindsey has been questioning you about the Serrano murder?" he asked before taking another bite of his hot dog.

"That's right," Heather said. "And speaking of questions, I have one for you, officer."

"This isn't about the murder case, is it? Because you know I can't discuss that."

"Well then, let me give you a hypothetical scenario. Suppose you were trying to track down information about a suspect and couldn't find out anything about the person, not a credit card or even a driver's license under their name before the person came to live in your town. And someone here tells you they were best friends in college, yet the name doesn't come up when you check the college year books for those years. Nor does a photo of that person. What would you think?"

"Simple." Sam shrugged. "The person changed their name and appearance."

"I figured that out," Heather said. "But what reason could they have for doing it?"

"Maybe they're hiding from someone," Chad suggested.

Heather suspected her aunt had been hiding from Jimmy the Horse ever since his prison sentence ended.

Sam glanced at Heather with a thoughtful look. "Or else they're in Federal Witness Protection."

"But how would an ordinary person, like myself, go about finding out that information?"

"You can't," Henderson said. "Why do you want to know?"

"Just a thought." Heather shrugged. *Well, there goes that line of inquiry.*

Officer Henderson stared into Heather's eyes. "If you know something about someone, you'd better tell Detective Lindsey, or you could be arrested for withholding information."

"I don't know anything," Heather lied. "Like I said, it was just a thought. But it's something you might look into by digging a little deeper into Serrano's past and seeing if there's someone who lives here he may have recognized. Or else, check for someone he'd recently swindled out of a lot of money."

Julia glanced at her cell phone, stood, and grabbed the white paper bags from the table. "Heather, our dinners are getting cold." She turned to the men. "It was nice chatting with you. But we have to be somewhere... like, right now."

Heather scrunched her nose and followed her aunt as Julia took a few steps toward the car. "Where do we have to be again?"

"You remember," Julia tilted her head. "At the..." Her large brown eyes went wide.

As usual, Heather didn't have a clue, but she went along with her aunt anyway. "Oh, right. We really do have to go," she said. "Good night, and thanks for the information." *What there was of it.*

"I still need to talk to you, Heather," Chad called after her. "Text me when you're free."

By the time she could respond to his request, Julia was out of sight. "Hey, wait up." Heather rushed around to the front of the hot dog stand. "I thought you wanted to eat outdoors this evening."

Julia stopped at the car and waited for Heather to catch up. "We'll have to eat on the way. Christine just texted me. Jimmy went out and was last seen entering the off-track betting facility. If I know him, and I do, he'll probably be there until they close. But I have to search his room while Christine's still at the front desk. And that'll only be for an hour or so."

Chapter 25

HEATHER wolfed down her dinner on the way to the hotel. She pulled her car into the parking lot, waiting for the heartburn to begin as she knew it would. And soon.

Putting the car into park, she turned to her aunt. "This is a bad idea. What could you possibly find in Jimmy's room that might incriminate him in Denny's murder?"

"I won't know until I look. But the cards told me, it's a go for today."

Heather wondered what was worse, the evil curse, or the card readings.

Julia got out of the car and rushed to the entrance of the hotel, where she waited for Heather. They walked in together. Christine, at the front desk, acknowledged them with a quick nod. Her light blue eyes scanned the lobby.

Several guests were coming in from the street entrance. A young couple stopped inside and faced the doors like they were waiting for someone. And three, well-dressed, middle-aged women went into the restaurant.

Without a word, Christine put her hand out toward Julia, palm down, holding, what Heather assumed, was the card key to Jimmy's room. Julia put her hand under Christine's, and a moment later, the card was out of sight. All very innocent-looking.

I wonder how long they practiced that trick?

"I'll text you when he comes in," Christine said, as if she and Julia were conducting some legitimate business.

Julia nodded and headed to the elevator.

When the doors opened, she walked in, and Heather rushed in after her. "Oh no, you're not leaving me in the lobby. Someone has to keep an eye on you."

"Then you can be my lookout."

What Heather wanted to do was talk her aunt out of searching the room and making her an accessory, but Julia was adamant, so what alternative did she have? At least this way, she'd have a modicum of control over the situation, so things wouldn't get out of hand.

A moment later, searing pain shot through Heather's chest. The heartburn she'd been expecting struck like a branding iron. She winced and pressed a hand to her chest as if that would relieve the pain.

"What's wrong," Julia asked as they emerged from the elevator.

"Heartburn." Heather could barely get the word out. "Do you have an antacid in your purse?"

"No, but if I remember correctly, Jimmy had acid reflux. If you're lucky, he still does, so there may be some in his room."

It was the last place Heather wanted to go, but what choice did she have? She followed her aunt to his door. Before Julia put the key card into the slot, she opened her purse and donned a pair of clear vinyl gloves.

She handed a pair to Heather. "Here, put these on."

Does she always carry clear gloves around? Heather had to wonder, but at this point, it didn't matter. She'd do anything to get rid of the pain in her chest. She slipped the gloves on and followed her aunt.

Inside Jimmy's room, Julia stopped near the door and glanced around. "Doesn't this look like the exact one we had when we stayed here?"

"I guess all the rooms look alike." Heather walked into the bathroom and checked the short shelf under the mirror. Shaving cream, razor, deodorant, but no antacids. She went into the bedroom as Julia opened the desk drawer.

"Have you found anything yet?"

Her aunt gasped as she pulled out a square piece of cardboard. Then she let out a sigh of pure sentiment, as if she'd just seen a cute kitten. This was an emotion Heather seldom, if ever, heard from her aunt.

"I found a photo of me in my younger days," Julia said. "I remember the day Jimmy took this with his Polaroid. We were on our way to a party at his friend's house. Just look at my beautiful auburn hair and my incredible figure. And my face. I was gorgeous. I looked a lot like you look now."

"An old picture?" Heather pressed hard at her chest. "I'm in agony." The pain was getting to her. It was hard to think of anything else. "I thought you'd found some antacids."

"Oh yeah." Julia fished two TUMS out of a large bottle in the drawer and handed them to her.

Heather hesitated before popping them into her mouth. "Do you think he'll notice they're missing?"

"From a big bottle like this?" Julia laughed. "Who counts antacid tablets?"

Heather popped them into her mouth, chewed, and swallowed. A few moments later, blessed relief.

"Sweet to think Jimmy's kept this photo all these years." Julia's voice cracked as she spoke, like she might break into tears.

"Put it back," Heather said. "And start looking for something incriminating."

Julia took the photo to the mirror and gazed at herself with the picture in one hand. Then with the other, she fluffed her wild, shoulder-length, fire-engine red hair. "You don't suppose Jimmy thinks I'll ever look like this again, do you?"

"Not unless you find the keys to a time machine hidden around here somewhere."

Julia tsked. "You're right." She took a deep breath. "Sentiment has no place in a murder investigation." She put the photo back and closed the drawer. "That's what Benny… I mean, Detective Lindsey told me when I tried to talk him into… Hmm."

Heather waited near the door as Julia searched the other drawers in the room. "There doesn't seem to be anything in plain sight I can use, so, like I said, it's time to go to the mattresses."

Heather shivered. "And like *I* said, this is *not* a *Godfather* movie." *My aunt had better not have a horse's head hidden out in the hallway somewhere.*

Julia raised the multi-colored spread from the side of the bed and flung it over the top. Then she lifted the mattress. "Hold this up so I can search underneath."

Heather stared at her a moment. *I've come this far. I might as well go all the way.*

She held the mattress while Julia stuck her hands in the space and slowly moved them from the top of the bed to the bottom.

She pulled out a small stash of money wrapped in a rubber band. "Look at this!"

Heather couldn't believe her aunt had actually found something.

He's as bad as my aunt. When I first met her here, that's how she carried her money. Only the wad was in her purse.

Julia took the rubber band off. Twenties unraveled and fell to the floor. "There's a small bottle of something here." She examined it and read the label. "It's a homeopathic remedy for stomach ulcers. One of the ingredients is belladonna. Extremely diluted and in very small doses, it can be used as a pain killer, but in large doses, it's poison."

Aunt Julia always surprised her.

"How do you know that?"

"I took a botany course in college that included poisonous plants."

"So that's how you knew about Deadly Nightshade. But didn't you say that belladonna was just one of the toxins in that plant?"

"How do we know this label is describing what's in the bottle? Might be something totally different."

"What are you doing?"

"I'm taking pictures of the label on this container, just in case I need it sometime." When she was done, Julia wrapped the money around the bottle with the rubber band, and put it back under the mattress.

Heather let the mattress down, and Julia made the bed.

"If the police consider Jimmy a suspect, I'm sure they would have already searched this room and found the medication," Heather said.

"They consider me a suspect, and they haven't searched our apartment."

Heather shrugged. "There were a lot of other people in the restaurant at the same time Denny and Jimmy were, who could also be considered suspects, including your three friends from the retirement village, along with the mayor, his accountant, Johnny Tanner, and Sylvia. And those are only the people we know of."

"But the others don't have a reason to kill Denny. Jimmy does."

"You don't know that for sure. There might be someone else with a motive. But if we're going to find out who, we might try looking at things from the perspective of the victim for a change."

"That's a good idea." Julia put her cell phone back in her purse. "I'm going to attempt to find out who Denny spoke to, or may have swindled, the week he was here before Jimmy came."

"Good. You do that. Now, let's go home."

Heather was never so glad to get out of a room in her life. Just the thought of Jimmy coming back and catching them made her heart flip, although this was not the first time they'd done this. She hoped it would have been less stressful this time, but it wasn't. With a sense of relief, she followed her aunt out into the hallway.

Julia pressed the button for the elevator. "I think it's time to think outside the box."

Chapter 26

As the elevator doors opened, Julia turned to Heather. "You can wait for me in the car. I want to stay behind and talk to Christine."

"No," Heather said as they made their way to the front desk. "I'll hang around the lobby." *I want to hear everything.*

As they approached, Christine stood behind the desk with her hand out, palm up. Julia placed hers on top, returning the key card.

"Thanks," Julia said. "One question, Chris. Did you see Denny get friendly with anyone at the hotel during the week he stayed here, before Jimmy joined him?"

Christine set the key card behind the counter. "He talked to a few other hotel guests, but it was a slow week and there weren't many. Then I saw him in the restaurant talking to some diners when I went in for lunch or dinner break. He seemed like a real friendly guy."

"Oh yes, Denny could be extremely friendly when he wanted something from you. Could you hear if he was talking about me?"

"From the little I was able to catch, some of it was about you, but it was also about someone else, someone he thought he knew. But who could Denny possibly know in this town if he'd never been here before? People get mistaken for other people all the time."

"Oh yes, I know," Julia said. "Detective Lindsey once called me by his ex-wife's name. Not that I resemble her in any way."

Heather and Christine exchanged glances. Julia and the detective's ex-wife, Gladys, could be twins.

"Denny said he had a picture of the person he was looking for on his cell phone. But he never got around to showing it to me."

"When they found Denny, there was no cell phone on him," Julia said.

Heather fingered her car key. "Maybe the killer stole it. Or maybe when Krystal was jogging around the bookstore on Sunday morning and came across Denny's body, she took his cell phone."

"Oh Heather, why would she want to do that?" Christine asked.

"He might have had some pictures of her doing something she shouldn't have been doing, and she needed to erase the photos."

"Did Denny spend a lot of time at her off-track betting place?" Julia asked.

"As far as I know, he did. But then, that's what gamblers come to this town for. What else is there to do here, unless he liked shopping at boutiques or fishing in the park lagoon?"

"Do you suppose Krystal kept his phone, assuming she had it in the first place?" Heather asked no one in particular. She turned to her aunt. "Was Denny into extortion or blackmail?"

"Denny and Jimmy were into a lot of things. But I think you're getting way off track here. They were more into the smalltime stuff."

"I don't think I am. Maybe Denny saw an opportunity to extort a lot of money from Krystal and decided to blackmail her for big bucks she may not have had, or wasn't willing to part with."

Julia pressed her lips together in a determined look. "She'd have the money to pay him as long as she still has the winning betting slip her father cheated me out of. It's worth nearly a hundred thou. All she has to do is cash it in."

"Maybe she doesn't know she has it." Heather surprised herself by defending Krystal. "She probably cleared out all of her father's things after he passed away."

Julia shook her head. "She knows. I'm sure of it. If you found a betting slip among your dead father's possessions, wouldn't you check it out?"

"I would, and if it was worth anything, I'd have cashed it in, so that's probably what she did. Besides, even if she still had the betting slip, there's no possible way you could prove it was your money that purchased it."

Julia leaned back against the front counter and looked down. She sighed in defeat. "I guess you're right. But that slip represented all the money I had in the world."

"I'm sorry you lost it letting Krystal's father bet on a horse for you, but that's what you get for giving all your money to a stranger."

"But I had my derringer too, and I let him know it. Until it was confiscated by the police when they found out about all my unpaid parking tickets." Julia looked up. "I don't trust banks, and like I told you, I was heading for your sister Emily's in Champaign to start over when the train broke down here. How could I have predicted something like that? Although the cards did forewarn of sorrow and great loss. I should have heeded the warning."

Christine put her hand on Julia's shoulder. "I'm glad your train broke down here, or I never would have met you. It's been such fun having you around."

Julia smiled at Christine. "I'm glad I met you too. I love having a partner in crime… I mean in solving them."

Instead of smiling back, Christine glanced past Julia, her eyes widening as her jaw dropped. "You two, get out, and hurry up! Jimmy the Horse is coming toward the front door."

By the time Heather and her aunt reached the back hallway, Jimmy was right behind them. The man had extremely long legs. "Julie, wait!"

Julia stopped as they reached the door.

Heather turned to her aunt. "I'll be in the car."

"Julia grabbed Heather's arm to stop her from moving. "No. You'll wait right here." Then she lowered her voice and added with a smile, "If you don't mind."

"I don't." Heather had the distinct impression her aunt didn't want to be alone with Jimmy.

She was sure Christine would be able to hear everything that was being said from where she stood in the lobby, which gave her a little reassurance in case it was something threatening.

"Where have you been?" Jimmy said in a jovial voice. "I've looked everywhere for you. When I went to your apartment she," he pointed to Heather, "told me you weren't home and probably wouldn't be for days. Then someone said you were doing community service at the retirement village, but no one there seems to know where you are at any given time."

Julia squared her drooping shoulders, giving her a look of confidence. "I move around a lot."

"And tonight, I find you in my hotel lobby. What a bit of luck, huh?"

"Yeah," Julia answered in a flat tone. "So, what do you want?"

He glared at her. "You know what I want. And I'll pester you until I get it."

"Just like you pestered Denny to death?"

Jimmy narrowed his eyes and gave her a sideways glance. "Denny was my friend. I didn't kill him."

Julia jabbed her index finger at Jimmy. "He was also your brother-in-law. You used him and probably hated him for what he did to your sister. You got rid of him so she could collect his insurance money. It would have been so easy to poison his breakfast on Sunday morning."

Heather rolled her eyes. *If this is Aunt Julia's way of getting Jimmy to confess to murder, I don't think it's going to work.*

Jimmy sucked in a breath. "Sure, he was my brother-in-law, and he was helping my sister the best he could. I didn't know he was poisoned. If he was, he probably felt sick and knocked on your back door for help, but instead of helping, you shoved him down the stairs."

"I did not." Julia huffed. "True, he probably felt sick, but he must have fallen on his own, because I never opened my back door. And even if I did open it, which I didn't, I had no reason to kill Denny, but you have plenty."

She hit the crash bar and opened the back door. "Come on Heather, we don't have to stay here and listen to any more from this..." she looked him up and down, "murderer. We're leaving."

Heather rushed outside, and Julia followed, letting the door slam behind her.

Jimmy swung it open again, stuck his head out, and yelled, "This isn't over, Jules! You *will* give me what I want."

Chapter 27

In the car on the way home, Jimmy's last words disturbed Heather to the point where she had to ask. "Okay, let's have it. What does Jimmy really want from you? And don't tell me it's just the two hundred thousand dollars."

"He also wants to marry me. But he's not going to get that either."

Heather pulled the Chevy into her parking space behind the bookstore. "I thought it might be something else."

She had a hard time believing her aunt, even though she did hear Jimmy propose to her.

Julia stepped out of the car and slammed the door. "That's all I'm going to say about it. Now, lets go upstairs. It's getting late, and I'm tired. We both have to get up early tomorrow."

Heather couldn't shake the nagging feeling that something didn't seem right about all this. As she laid her uneasy head on the pillow that night, her jumbled thoughts tried to make sense of what was going on between her aunt and Jimmy.

Her cell phone pinged. She rolled over and glanced at the text message from Chad.

We have to talk.

He must be angry with her for fixing up his sister with Jack. *Should I face him? Or just pretend I didn't get it?*

Her phone pinged again. *Please. It's important.*

Maybe if she ignored him long enough, he'd forget about it.

Only he wouldn't. *The man is an ex P.I. He's tenacious.*

"If I don't answer, I'll never get to sleep tonight thinking about it." She texted him back. *Ok. When?*

Pick u up 12:30. City Hall. Tomorrow

After a few moments of staring into the darkness of her room, considering the consequences of her actions, she finally rested her head on the pillow. She thought of every possible excuse for fixing Ashley up with Jack behind Chad's back. But how could she lie to the man she loved? It was too painful to even think about. *I don't want to lose Chad now, just when we've found each other.*

A tear fell from her eye and rolled down her cheek.

Heather spent the morning in her little office, trying her best to work on her budget without thoughts of what she'd say to Chad interrupting every few minutes, but the claustrophobia was getting to her. The office had started out as a small storage room, and it shrank a little every day as more banker's boxes were shoved along the walls during the night.

Right now, she had just enough room to pass in front of the boxes to get to her desk with four feet of space to move her chair.

She'd gone for a coffee break at ten, and the next time she glanced at the clock, it was nearly 12:30. Swallowing back bitter tears at the thought that Chad may never speak to her again, she picked up her purse and slipped into her stilettos, grateful to get out of the stuffy room for a while.

Then she locked her office door and made her way outside, rubbing her bottom lip with her thumbnail as nerves about her upcoming conversation with Chad got the better of her.

Once outside, she spotted his Lexus, and her heart quickened.

He got out of the car and met her on the sidewalk. "Hi."

She gave him a weak smile and nodded her greeting. "Where are we going for lunch?"

He pointed to the brown brick building a few doors down. "Just over to the deli. I have to get back to the store soon, but I promised I'd bring something back for Ashley."

Once they'd ordered and received their corned beef on rye and sodas, Chad made his way to the corner of the room, where a table had just been vacated.

"Let's sit here." He sat and took a deep breath, not touching his food. "I don't know how to put this, so I'll just say it. Your ex has been on a date with my sister, and I'm worried about her dating a man like Jack."

Chad was serious.

A laugh bubbled up from inside, she was so relieved. Heather placed her hand over her mouth to suppress a smile and scrunched her eyes in an effort to make them look serious.

"How did you find out about this... date?" She asked from the grin behind her hand.

Chad leaned back in his seat and crossed his arms. "That's the worst part. Krystal sent me a string of text messages about Jack having dinner with Ashley at The

Vendeglo. Then she left a bunch of selfies she took of them with hearts and said I could thank her for letting me know later. At her house." Chad huffed. "I wish she'd stay out my life."

At least he's not mad at me. Only because he didn't know the whole story. But she wasn't going to press her luck.

"This was probably a one-time thing. Jack has no intention of staying in town. I doubt if he'll ask her out again." *As a matter of fact, I know he won't.* "Besides, even if she did go to dinner with him once, you know Ashley's heart is with Miklos."

"You're right. You don't suppose she was just trying to make him jealous, do you?"

Heather looked to the side in a thoughtful manner. "That's a good possibility."

<><><>

After they'd eaten and were about to leave the deli, Chad reached into his pants pocket, pulled out a credit card, and dragged an old playing card out along with it.

"Before I forget. I fished this ace of spades out of our swimming pool this morning. I believe it's one of your aunt's. Makki must have stolen it the other night when Julia told Ashley's fortune. It's his favorite thing to do in the summer, dropping items he's stolen into the swimming pool. I'm sorry to say, the card's been soaked. I dried it the best I could, but it's coming apart, and there are a few cat teeth marks. Please tell your aunt I'll replace her entire deck."

"I will." Heather shoved the card into her purse and didn't think any more of it.

Out on the street, she turned to Chad. "Thanks for lunch. Hope we can do it again sometime."

He smiled. "I look forward to it."

She returned his smile. Then she leaned in to kiss him and just as their lips met, she made an awkward turn, tripped on her heels, and stumbled back to City Hall. *That was real graceful.*

Just as Heather reached the heavy front door, it swung open, nearly clipping her shoulder. Startled, she took a few steps back. Marty Engels, the mayor's accountant, ran past her without a word before jumping into his jeep, parked in front of the building. He backed up and headed around the corner.

"Where's he going in such a hurry? Could he be the other person in town Denny thought he recognized and asked Christine about? He was at the restaurant Sunday. He might be the murderer." She jumped into her car as her mind raced, and barely managed to follow him at a discreet distance as the jeep wove in and out of what little traffic there was at this time of day, until he reached a part of town with neat rows of small, well-kept bungalows, each a little different from the others, with a wide driveway separating the houses. He turned into the driveway of a plain beige and brown brick with five cement steps and a white metal railing leading to the front door.

He got out of his car and ran up the stairs. Heather drove around the corner and parked across the street a few houses away. She slunk down behind the steering wheel and waited. For what, she had no idea.

A few moments later, a dark-haired woman driving a black Dodge Charger pulled up and parked in front of the house. Heather grabbed her cell and took photos of the statuesque woman in the forest green business suit as she got out of her car and rang the doorbell. Heather couldn't see who answered, but the woman was invited in. She snapped a photo of the Charger and the license plate.

She debated whether or not to sneak around the house and take a peek inside, when a black Chevy Tahoe pulled into the driveway, and two men, one tall and muscular and one short and slim, both wearing dark suits, got out and made their way to the front door, which was opened by the mysterious woman in green. Heather couldn't pass up the opportunity to take more photos. What was going on in there?

Whatever it is, I'd better not hang around.

Still slumped behind the wheel, she turned on the engine and raised her head to take a peek at the street. All clear, so she gunned it and sped past the house.

Dragging herself up as she reached the corner, she caught a glimpse of the two men in her rearview mirror. They stood on the sidewalk in front of the house, holding their cell phones to their ears, and staring after her car. Beads of sweat formed on her upper lip.

Heather jumped at the sound of her business cell ringing. She glanced at the phone on the passenger's seat to check the caller ID.

Sylvia?

Chapter 28

HEATHER made her way back to City Hall without answering the call. She didn't want to stop in case those men were following her. But luck was with her this afternoon. Every light was green, and traffic seemed to have vanished. She finally parked in front of the old building, pulled out her business phone, and emailed the photos to herself at home, then deleted them all. She let out a deep breath of relief and made her way to her office door.

As she put her key in the lock, Sylvia approached her. "Where have you been? I've been trying to reach you." A slight wrinkle creased her usually smooth brow.

"I've been at lunch."

The wrinkle deepened. "Don't you answer your phone?"

"Not when I'm driving."

Sylvia shook her head, and the wrinkle disappeared. "The mayor wants to see you in his office. Right now!"

Heather made her way to Mayor Bandyk's office. *I'd better pull myself together before I go in there.* She took a quick breath, put on a smile, and knocked on his closed door.

"Come in."

She swung the door open and sauntered in, still smiling. "You wanted to see me, Mr. Mayor?"

"Ah, Miss Stanton." He got up from his desk to meet her in the middle of the room. "Please close the door."

She did, and as she turned back around, he was right in her face.

He lowered his voice. "I just wanted to inform you that Madam Z had a massive stroke in her jail cell last night and passed away. The court has made the decision to close the case against her."

Heather was relieved at Madam Z's passing, and happy she wouldn't have to testify against her at the trial.

"But what about her brother, Bax? Is he still at large?"

"I'm sorry to say, he is. But it's just a matter of time until he's caught and prosecuted for his crimes."

That news sent a shiver down Heather's spine. She wouldn't want to run into Bax on a dark night. He and his sister, Madam Z, had kidnapped her and her aunt two weeks ago, and threatened to kill them.

"How's your assignment coming along?" the mayor asked. "Have you come up with a budget yet?"

She had only a few more places to check, but just to be on the safe side, she said, "You'll have it by 9:00 tomorrow morning."

"Good. I'll look it over and let you know if it's acceptable." He reached into his jacket pocket and pulled out several business cards which he handed to her. "Feel free to hand these out if anyone gives you flack."

Along with the cards, a small vial had fallen to the floor. Heather recognized the container as one of Madam Z's Special Elixir bottles.

The mayor stooped down to pick it up. He looked up at Heather. She couldn't help staring at it. "Yes, it's one of her elixirs. She made it for me to relieve stress, and, believe it or not, it worked. But it's empty now." He tossed it in his trash can. "I think just about everyone in town went to see Madam Z at one time or other for help with a problem."

"I'm sure she talked many people into buying her elixirs, sir. She was almost Machiavellian in the way she dealt with the public."

"Yes, I have to agree." The mayor walked back to his desk. "But enough about Madam Z. Sylvia has made arrangements for all of the unwanted files in the building to be shredded. I need you to point them out to the driver. And check with the other departments, so no one can complain they didn't know about it. I'll leave you to coordinate everything."

"Yes, sir. Is that all you wanted to see me about?" She expected him to say, yes, so she made her way to the door.

But before she could open it, he said, "Just one more thing. Someone told me you were parked on the eight hundred block of Alpine Street around one this afternoon. Is this true?"

"Yes, I was." There was no reason to lie about it.

"And what were you doing there, if I may be so bold as to ask?"

What would Aunt Julia say?

She hesitated a moment as she tried to think like her aunt, and an idea popped into her head. "I was driving around town on my lunch hour, looking for a nice neighborhood where my aunt might consider buying a house. And I came across Alpine Street with some lovely-looking old bungalows, so I stopped to get a better look at the houses." She let out a breath.

He put his hand out, palm up. "Can I see your business cell, please?"

"Of course." She handed it to him as heat rose to her face.

She couldn't see what he was doing, but it involved a lot of screen-tapping. *Good thing I got rid of those photos.* Of course, he had every right to do anything he wanted to the cell since it was the property of City Hall.

He handed it back to her. "I would advise you to stay away from that particular neighborhood. It's not desirable, and the houses are extremely overpriced. I know for a fact your aunt would not want to live there."

"Thanks for the tip. I'll look elsewhere, I guess."

"I would appreciate it if you didn't mention anything you saw there to anyone. Ever. Do we understand each other?"

Heather nodded. "Yes, sir."

He waved a hand at her and gave her that practiced, enigmatic smile. "You may go."

She made her way to the door and swung it open, the warmth still burning her cheeks. She hated being dismissed with a wave of his hand like she was a servant. *I don't care if he* is *the mayor.*

Heather scurried down the hall, and into her office. As she leaned against the closed door, she paged through her business cell. Maybe she was just being paranoid over this guy. There was probably a good explanation for everything. *I just have to find out what it is.*

Beads of sweat had formed on her forehead. She needed something cold to drink, preferably with sugar and caffeine to help her focus.

Heather made her way to the basement break room where numerous vending machines containing everything from cold sandwiches sealed in plastic to fresh fruit stood against the walls. She sauntered up to the drink machine and selected a can of Pepsi, and then she got herself a bag of Peanut M&Ms for later.

She made her way to the hall to catch the elevator, but when the doors opened, the mayor's accountant emerged.

Their eyes met.

Heather's breath caught.

Marty barged his way out of the elevator, making her step back, and continued toward her until she was up against the wall. His beady eyes bulged as he glared at her.

"Who are you? What are you doing here? And what do you want from me?"

His questions came in such rapid succession, every thought went out of her mind. "I… I'm Heather Stanton. I work for the mayor. I don't want anything from you."

By this time, they were practically nose to nose. "Then why are you following me?"

His garlic breath made her eyes tear. "I'm not." She had to look away.

"Then why were you parked across the street from my house today taking pictures?"

She couldn't help scrunching her face. *Now he'll be able to read me, and he'll know I'm lying.* "I didn't know it was your house. I just liked the neighborhood, and I hoped one of the houses might be for sale."

An elevator dinged. She released her breath as the doors opened, and Sylvia strolled out. Her eyes must have detected the fear in Heather's.

"What's going on here?'

Marty backed off and strolled in the direction of the men's room around the corner.

Sylvia glanced after him. "What a jerk. What did he do to you?"

She didn't want to get Sylvia involved in this, so she said, "It was just a misunderstanding."

"I don't like that guy," Sylvia said. "He's rude and smug. I don't care how big his problems are, they're no excuse for bad behavior."

"He has big problems?"

Sylvia rubbed the back of her neck then motioned Heather to a corner of the break room, where she brought her voice down to a whisper. "Like I told you, the walls here are very thin and I hear a lot. All I can say is, whatever he's mixed up in, you'd be better off to stay away from him."

Heather put a hand on Sylvia's tense shoulder to reassure her. "I'll be careful in the future."

"For whatever reason this guy is working here, the mayor has made the best of it and has used the man's accounting talents to get what he wants, like he does with everyone who works for him."

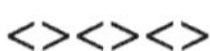

Heather went back to her office. *I knew there had to be a logical explanation for his rudeness.* With the accountant off her mind, she began working on the budget again. While she hated number crunching, it had to be done by the end of the day.

At four, Heather went over the figures one more time. Then she closed and saved the confidential file on the computer and emailed it to the mayor so he'd have it by 9:00 a.m.

She'd check with the other departments tomorrow morning to make sure everyone who needed to get their papers shredded got their boxes to her office before the truck arrived.

With the budget for this dance finally done, except for a few small exceptions which she needed to talk to the mayor about, Heather breathed a sigh of relief as she got into her car. She looked forward to having a nice, relaxing evening at home—putting her feet up with a glass of White Zinfandel before her aunt arrived. She hoped Julia hadn't finished it all.

Her cell phone rang.

Chapter 29

HEATHER answered the phone. "Hi, Aunt Julia."

"I've been talking to residents in the retirement village," Julia said. "And some people I encountered outside on my lunch hour. I was trying to trace Denny's steps when he was here that week before Jimmy came. It seems he was noticed by a lot of folks because of his unusual choice of shoes. While he did a lot of talking, or questioning I should say, he didn't try to swindle any of them out of their life savings. At least not the ones I talked to, so that theory is out for now. But Christine Talan said he did spend an inordinate amount of time at the off-track betting facility."

"You couldn't wait to tell me until I got home?"

"That's just the point. I need you to do something for me on the way. Would you be a dear and stop at the off-track betting place to question the people who work there?"

Heather couldn't believe her aunt's request. "About what?"

"Ask if they heard Denny or Jimmy offering to sell shares of a brand new venture that seemed 'too good to be true.'"

"You mean like a Ponzi scheme?"

"See, I knew you'd pick up on it. You're so intelligent and so sweet for doing this for me."

And so obliging. "Really, Aunt Julia, I don't want to go there and possibly have another run-in with Krystal. The last time she almost had us arrested."

"Just avoid her. She can't be everywhere at once. Please. You know I've been banned from going in there. And I need to get something else on Jimmy if I'm going to get him to confess to Denny's murder."

Heather huffed. What else could she do? Her aunt always knew how to push her buttons. Besides, she wanted to see if Krystal had Denny's cell phone. "All right. I'll give it a shot."

And so she turned the car in the direction of the off-track betting facility. Heather hadn't been there since before the renovation.

The outside looked much more inviting, with it's wood slats painted a bright white and a navy and white striped metal awning over the door. Three neon horses ran a continuous race in the window, and the letters OTB were painted in black above the racing horses.

She parked across the street and walked up to the new oak door. Johnny Tanner, Krystal's accountant, stood in front of her with his legs spread apart and his arms folded over his shallow chest.

"Excuse me." She tried to get past him, but his body blocked her in every direction she moved.

"I'd like to go inside please," she said in her most authoritative voice.

He glanced over his shoulder. She couldn't see who he was looking at, but she had a feeling it was Krystal. "Sorry, we're at capacity," he said in his tinny-sounding voice. "I can't let you in."

This was the first time she'd ever encountered something like this, and she wasn't expecting it. Gathering her thoughts, she said, "Oh, then I'll wait here until someone comes out."

He began to close the door but stopped halfway. "It might be a long time. Just go home. We don't want no vagrants hangin' round outside. It'll give our other customers the wrong idea about the place."

"Hey, I'm not a vagrant," she yelled at him as he closed the door in her face.

How rude! I guess Aunt Julia's not the only one who's been banned from this establishment.

Insulting Heather only made her more determined to get inside. She went around to the alley to size up the back of the building. She'd gotten in this way once before. But the old wooden door had been changed to a sturdy metal one. She turned the handle and pulled and then pushed, but it was locked. White wood shutters now covered the window, so there was no peeking inside to see what was going on. There appeared to be a new alarm system too, and two security cameras stuck out from strategic positions on the building.

"Guess I'll try to get in again tomorrow." *On the off-chance Krystal might change her mind or won't be around.* She waved to a security camera and left.

As soon as she entered the living room, her aunt was on her.

"So, what did you find out?"

"Nothing. I couldn't get in."

"Why not?"

"Johnny Tanner was guarding the door, and he told me they were at capacity, and he couldn't possibly let anyone else inside. I'm sure Krystal told him to insist I go home. Guess you're not the only one who's not welcome there."

Julia plopped down on the sofa. "There goes that idea."

"Not necessarily." Heather put her purse on the end table and opened it. *After the day I've had, I need some chocolate.*

She grabbed the bag of Peanut M&Ms and offered some to her aunt.

Julia smiled and put her hand out. "What's on your mind?"

"I still might be able to get inside when Krystal's not there." Heather poured a few into her aunt's hand and popped one into her mouth.

"But how will you know when she's not?" Julia asked.

"I've been thinking about asking Jack to take her out to dinner as a favor to me. Somehow, I don't think he'd need much encouragement. But then, I don't really want to be in Jack's debt for anything."

"Getting Krystal out of the place is a good idea, but Johnny Tanner will still be guarding the door."

"You're right." Heather popped two M&Ms into her mouth and chewed while she considered her options.

Julia jumped to her feet. "I know! We'll consult the cards and see what they have to say." She went into her room and came out with the deck of playing cards she seemed to always have with her. She spread the cards out, getting the deck ready to be cleansed for a new reading.

Heather went to her purse and grabbed the ruined card Chad had given her.

"I almost forgot to tell you, Makki stole your ace of spades the other day when we were at Christine's for dinner and dropped it in the Willows' swimming pool." She held the split card up and looked it over.

Julia gasped. "Thanks, I'll take it." Her hand was almost quicker than Heather's eye as she snatched the ace from her hand and shoved it between the sofa cushions. "But now my good deck is ruined. And everything they'd predicted for me was wrong."

Julia flung the rest of the cards down. "No wonder things haven't been going my way since that dinner."

"You've been relying an awful lot on those cards lately." Heather went around to the back of the sofa and noticed the damaged ace stuck between the cushions behind her aunt. She pulled it out and held it up.

"What's this all about?" Heather demanded. "And don't try to fluff it off as nothing. I'm not going to let it go until you tell me."

Julia looked at her and scooped up the cards from the coffee table. "I really didn't want to get you involved, but I guess I don't have a choice."

Heather perched on the sofa next to her. "Okay, let's have it."

Chapter 30

"It's a long story." Julia rubbed her forehead. "I'm getting a headache just thinking about it. And I don't know where to begin."

Heather stared at her, patiently waiting for another one of her aunt's outrageous stories.

"I guess I'll start with an explanation about certain decks of playing cards that were around in World War II."

"World War II?" Heather leaned back on the sofa to get comfortable. "This *is* going to be a long story."

Julia scrunched her eyes in a look of annoyance. "It's not as if I was around then. I'm just relaying to you how it was told to me. There were certain decks of playing cards sent to American soldiers who were being held in POW camps throughout Europe. These cards were inside the Special Christmas packages given to them by the Red Cross.

"When the cards got wet, they peeled apart and disclosed a secret escape map. Once the map pieces were revealed, all the POW had to do was assemble the cards in the right order to get the full map to navigate his way back to the Allies. The U.S. Playing Card Company teamed up with British and American intelligence agencies to create those cards so downed pilots and captured soldiers could find the Allied lines."

"But didn't the camp guards get suspicious?"

"Evidently, playing cards were common among the troops. They didn't suspect a thing. No one knows for sure how many decks were produced, but the only two known surviving decks are in the International Spy Museum in Washington, D.C."

"So what does this have to do with *your* cards?" Heather's stomach flipped as an idea crossed her mind. "Don't tell me you stole one of the decks."

Julia shook her head. "Of course not! Will you be quiet and let me finish? There's a third deck that only a couple of people knew about. A very valuable deck." Julia pointed to the cards on the table.

Heather glanced at the layout. "They look like ordinary playing cards to me."

"That's the point. They're supposed to," Julia said. "I carry them with me all the time and use them *only* for my Cartomancy readings. I'm always careful with them."

Heather sucked in a breath as it dawned on her. "Because they peel apart, and there's a section of map underneath some of the cards?"

"No. That's not how these particular playing cards work."

"So what makes this deck more valuable?"

"Because the map embedded in these cards leads to a cache of precious jewels that in today's market could be worth millions."

Of all the stories her aunt had told, Heather found this one the hardest to believe. "Even if this map did lead to some jewels, how do you know they're still there?

Someone might have found them by now. World War II was a long time ago."

"I'm not going to take the chance of letting Jimmy get the cards with the map in case the jewels are still there."

"If the cards are so valuable, why don't you keep them in a safety deposit box at a bank?"

"Are you kidding? Banks are always closing or being taken over by other banks. I don't trust them, never did. And the way I travel around the country, I'd rather keep them with me. At least I know where they are, and Jimmy can't get his grubby hands on them."

"Okay," Heather said. "Let's say the jewels *are* there, and you find them some day. You can't keep anything that was originally stolen."

Julia shook her head. "They weren't."

"How do you that know for sure?"

"I just do. But that's a whole other story."

"Heather crossed her arms. "I'd love to hear it, because I have nothing better to do with my time."

A sudden knock on the door made her shoulders jump to her ears.

Julia leapt from the sofa. "Who could that be?"

"You don't suppose it's Jimmy, do you?" With a trembling hand, Heather opened her purse and pulled out the pepper spray, just in case.

Scooping up the cards from the table, Julia held them in her hand and sauntered to the door. "Who is it?"

"It's Chad."

Heather dropped her shoulders and she let out a breath as Julia opened it.

"I hope I'm not bothering you," he said, "but I wanted to give you this."

He opened his hand and revealed a new deck of playing cards. Julia took it with her free hand. "Thanks. But why?"

"To replace the deck Makki ruined."

Julia invited him to come in and sit down. "Would you like something to drink?"

"No thanks. I can't stay."

Julia knelt at the coffee table and laid the deck she carried on it. Then she opened the cellophane on the new deck and slipped the cards out of the box.

"They look almost exactly the same. Except for a couple things."

Chad leaned over to take a look. "All the playing cards for sale at the drug store were pretty much standard, either red or blue. I remembered yours were blue. I felt bad about Makki ruining your deck."

Julia let out a chuckle. "I don't believe it."

"What's so funny?" Chad asked.

"The fact that you went to the trouble of buying me a replacement deck of cards tickles me," Julia said. "Thank you. It was a very nice gesture on your part."

"You're welcome," Chad said.

"There's something I want to show you." Julia went through all the face cards in the new deck. She pulled out the ace of spades and set it on the coffee table. Then she laid her ruined ace down next to it. "They're almost exactly the same, except the new card has a matte coating. Mine is shiny. That's because my cards were printed around or before the nineteen forties."

Heather leaned over to check the cards. "How do you know when they were printed?"

"There's a code on the ace of spades at the very bottom in tiny numbers that tells you approximately when the cards were manufactured. My grandmother gave me this deck, and she told me she acquired it right after the war. My ace has the code A1615, which means it had to be manufactured on or before the forties."

Heather picked up the new ace. "This card has a group of ten numbers and letters at the bottom. What does that tell us about when it was manufactured?"

Julia shrugged. "I have no idea about these new cards. You'll have to look it up."

Heather picked up her cell phone to do just that, when she noticed the time. "It's nearly six. Don't you have to close the bookstore, Chad?" Much as she hated to see him leave, she had to find out what her aunt was willing to tell him, in case her story about the map showing the location of the jewels was real. Not that she didn't trust Chad, but the fewer people who knew about it, the better.

"Oh yeah," he said. "I've got to get going." He pushed himself off the sofa. "I have a confession. I didn't just come up to give you the cards. I wanted to invite you both to dinner. Say around seven? I'll grill some steaks."

"Steak sounds great," Heather said. "We'd love to."

She was hungry and there was nothing left to eat in their apartment, except sardines and peanut butter and jelly. Also, she didn't want to be home in case Jimmy decided to show up on their doorstep again tonight.

"And thanks again for the new cards," Julia yelled after him.

Once the door latch clicked, Heather rushed over to her aunt, who was gathering up the playing cards. "Are you planning to tell Chad and Ashley about the map?"

Julia slid the cards back into their respective packages. "Only if the conversation comes around to the subject. And then, it'll be on a need-to-know basis. That is, if I think they need to know anything."

Chapter 31

HEATHER'S T-bone steak had been grilled to perfection, and she ate every bit of it, along with a side salad and a baked potato smothered in butter and sour cream. Just as she finished the last bite, Christine Talan sauntered into the Willows' back yard, carrying a covered cake plate.

"Hi, everyone. I hope I'm not disturbing you."

"Not at all," Chad said. He'd finished eating his dinner before Heather, so he got up from the table and walked over to Christine. "I'll take that."

Christine handed him the cake. "Thanks. I'm so glad you're finished with dinner, because I made this Black Forest cake for George's homecoming, but when he got back from his annual physical this afternoon, he told me the doctor said he had to go on a diet. He has to cut out white flour and sugar, so he's only eating fruit for dessert. But he wants me to go on the diet with him. Says he'll never do it alone." She touched the slight bulge at her waist. "Guess I could lose a few pounds too. I didn't know what to do with the cake, so I brought it over for you to enjoy."

"Thanks," Ashley peeked under the plate cover. "It's one of my favorites. What's George doing now?"

"He dusted off that old treadmill in the basement and says he's going to walk for the next hour, if he can last that long."

Chad picked up the cake plate and went toward the back door of the house. "Guess I'll cut the cake and make coffee. Come in when you're ready for dessert."

Christine glanced from person to person. "So, what's going on? Did I miss anything? I heard what Jimmy said to you at the hotel last night, Julia. Absolutely disgraceful. How could he think you'd sink so low as to murder Denny Serrano?"

Ashley's eyes widened. "Bring me up to speed."

Julia began to explain what happened, but Heather said, "I think I'll go in the kitchen and see how Chad's doing with dessert."

She didn't want to stick around for a recap of what went on. Besides, she'd only cringe at the excuse her aunt came up with as to why they were at the hotel last night. Julia couldn't possibly tell Ashley it was to illegally search Jimmy's room for evidence that *he* murdered Denny Serrano.

Heather opened the back door to the large, rectangular kitchen of her dreams, with its oak cabinets, stainless steel appliances, and huge center island with a double sink. Standing behind it was the *man* of her dreams. *What a perfect picture.*

The scent of freshly brewed coffee brought her down from the clouds.

"Having cake and coffee?" Chad asked.

She nodded, and he passed her a plate and an empty mug. Actually, she was stuffed, but right now she needed the chocolate in the cake and the caffeine in the coffee for courage to ask him a favor.

He filled her mug from the tall ten cup coffee maker on the counter, and she cut herself a slim slice of cake, then perched on one of the stools on the other side of the marble countertop.

"How's your aunt coming along with her investigation into Denny's murder?" he asked.

"She's trying to retrace his steps for the week before Jimmy arrived, in case he did something that might have offended someone enough to want to kill him. But it seems he spent a lot of time at the off-track betting facility. So, I've been attempting to help her by seeing if he gave anyone else a motive."

Chad perched on the stool next to her, coffee mug in hand. "Have you come up with anything new to report to the police?"

"I tried to get into the facility this afternoon, but Johnny Tanner guarded the door like a bulldog. He told me they were at capacity, and he couldn't possibly let anyone else in, and then he insisted I go home. I think Krystal told him to keep me out. So, I couldn't find out from the employees or the customers if Denny had been trying to sell them shares in some new Ponzi scheme. Or even search Krystal's office for Denny's cell phone."

"Woah!" Chad said. "What was that last part about searching Krystal's office?"

"I think Krystal grabbed Denny's cell phone Sunday morning when she discovered him."

"That's quite an assumption. What makes you consider that?"

"Don't you think it was awfully convenient for her to jog around the corner of your bookstore just in time to find him lying at the bottom of the stairs?"

"Well, yes I do. But I would assume the person who killed Denny also took his cell phone so as not to be incriminated."

"How do you know Krystal wasn't that person? He might have been blackmailing her for doing something illegal, in which case her livelihood would have been gone, and she would face jail time. Or he could have been extorting money from her, just because he thought he could get away with it."

Chad picked up his empty plate and set it in the sink. "You don't know Krystal like I do. She's too much of a coward to commit murder."

Heather followed him to the sink with her empty plate and cup. "As my aunt once told me, everyone has a point of no return when they're pushed too far and they lose control."

He chuckled. "I don't think Krystal could be pushed that far. But it sounds like something a hothead like Johnny Tanner might do." He gazed into Heather's eyes. "Don't you think we should leave this to the police? It might be dangerous asking questions alone."

He checked the wall clock. "Maybe you need help. It's after eight. I could still make it there before they close, and I might find out a few things."

You saved me the embarrassment of having to ask. Heather sighed. *We are so in sync.*

She put her arms around Chad's neck and gazed into his eyes. "Thank you. My aunt and I really appreciate this."

He leaned in and placed a warm, passionate kiss on her lips, but just when things were getting interesting, the back door opened. His sister wheeled herself in, followed by Julia and Christine, all chatting at the same time.

"Oh, sorry," Julia said. "Did we interrupt something?"

Heather took her arms down. "I was just telling Chad how we appreciate that he's going to the off-track betting facility to ask the questions you wanted me to ask."

Chad checked his cell phone. "I'd better get a move on if I want to get there before they close."

Heather followed him out the back door. "Wait. I'm going with you."

"But you said Tanner wouldn't let you in."

"The front door, no. But you can let me in the back door."

"Why?"

"So I can look for Denny's cell phone in Krystal's office."

"Assuming she has it. But what if she keeps it at her house?"

"I'll worry about that if I can't find it at the office. But if I *do* find it, there might be proof I can take to the police that she may have killed Denny."

"That kind of proof won't be admissible in court, you know."

"I don't care. At least I can get the police to look for other suspects besides my aunt."

Chad raised his arms in a gesture of defeat. "Fine. We'll do this your way."

Which is just the way Heather liked things done.

Chapter 32

CHAD parked around the corner from the off-track betting facility. Heather opened the car door to get out when he stopped her. "Wait." He grabbed a large, black hoodie from the back seat. "Put this on, so if you're caught on a security camera, they won't recognize you."

Heather put the hoodie on—it nearly touched her knees—and inhaled the clean, freshly laundered scent. She pulled the hood over her head and went to the alley while Chad walked around the corner to the front door. She assumed he'd gotten in because he didn't come around the back or text her. So she waited in an area of the alley where she was sure none of the security cameras could pick her up.

It was a mild June evening, and other than the stench from the garbage cans, it wasn't an unpleasant wait at first. But after fifteen minutes, her legs had gotten numb, and the putrid smell nauseated her.

"What's he doing in there?"

A lock being unlatched on the back door got her attention. She rushed up to it, turned the knob, and slowly pushed it open. Then she stuck her head inside.

The brightly lit back room of the establishment looked about the same size as the last time she'd been there.

They hadn't done much to it except slap a new coat of beige paint on the walls and replace the old brown floor tiles with ones that looked like Grecian marble. But they did add one thing that hadn't been there before—a large wooden octagonal card table with a green felt top and eight matching wooden chairs. *This reeks of illegal card games.*

She stepped inside and slowly closed the door behind her, trying not to make any noise, but it didn't matter. There was enough racket coming from the main gambling room to cover any sound she made back here. She walked down a short hallway to the end, where the door to Nikos' office was located, probably now taken over by Krystal. Heather shuddered at the unpleasant memories associated with the room. She closed her eyes a moment to ramp up her courage, took a deep breath, and knocked.

No answer.

She listened at the door but heard nothing except the vibration from her cell phone. A text from Chad: *U ok?*

She opened the office door, went inside, and closed it behind her. She texted a short reply.

In the office. Keep K busy.

He didn't text her back.

Why did this worry her?

Luckily the light was on in the office. The room had been completely redone with modern furniture, a large flat computer screen on a gray metal desk, a few awkward-looking plastic chairs in an odd color of pink, a small chrome refrigerator, and a white leather sofa against the back wall.

She rushed to the desk and opened the only drawer. Not much in there except a few office supplies and...

"What's this?" From the back of the drawer, she pulled out a small bottle of Madam Z's Special Elixir and read the label out loud. "Is good for what is bad."

Those were the same words printed on all the other bottles she'd seen, but it didn't explain what was in the potion. None of them did. She pulled out the stopper but hesitated before taking a whiff. The last one she opened smelled like shoe polish and made her eyes tear up. She took a cautious sniff. Sweet, slightly musky. She wouldn't be surprised if it was a love potion Madam Z brewed up for Krystal. But why would she do that? Krystal hated her. She blamed Madam Z for her mother's death. Maybe it was a peace offering? Or maybe it was Johnny Tanner's. It could be why Sylvia was dating a man like him. She couldn't think of any other reason.

Heather shoved the cork in and put the potion back in the drawer. Then she focused on her mission. *If I was Krystal, where would I put a cell phone that I'd just stolen?*

She checked behind the sofa and around the floor for Krystal's purse. No other places to store it, except... *The closet.*

The sliding closet doors were painted the same odd color of pink as the furniture and measured nearly the length of the room. Heather slid the door open about a foot and peered inside. There was plenty of standing room, so she squeezed in, hoping Krystal's purse was there.

Inside, the cedar walls smelled of her childhood. They'd had a closet made of cedar where her mother stored their winter coats. But this closet was mostly empty, except for two jackets on hangers and a high shelf where a few small corrugated boxes sat. She checked inside. The boxes were empty.

On a hook behind the jackets, a Givenchy gray quilted shoulder bag hung from a gold chain.

"Gorgeous." She turned it over to inspect it. "This has to sell for at least two thousand." She couldn't help admiring the workmanship. "What I wouldn't give to be able to afford a purse like this again."

Heather carefully opened the front flap and stuck her hand inside. *Lipstick, compact, a small brush, some tissues ... no phone.*

The office doorknob clicked, and footsteps sounded on the tile floor. Letting go of the purse, she pressed herself against the part of the closet door that was closed, shoving the two jackets in front of the narrow opening.

"Yeah, we were cellmates at Western Illinois Correctional for a year, until I got paroled," Johnny Tanner said.

"So that's how you knew Denny?" Jimmy replied.

"Yeah, but ain't it a coincidence after twenty years we should run into each other in this town? Hey, they don't know I'm an ex-con here. I burned my bridges behind me. As far as anyone knows, I'm an upstanding, respected businessman, so keep your trap shut if you know what's good for ya."

"Don't worry," Jimmy said. "I'm an ex-con too."

"I got myself a real goldmine here," Tanner said. "That clueless woman don't know nothing about runnin' a business like this. I got her so scared, she won't make a move unless I give the okay. Denny wanted in. But I straightened him out real quick."

There was a moment of silence, and then Tanner said, "Don't think you can horn in on my business either."

Heather's body was stiff with fear. She tried to reach for her cell phone, but she couldn't move.

"Don't worry about me," Jimmy said. "I'm not interested in this place. I'm after something totally different."

"Good," Tanner said. "When Denny left here on Sunday morning, he said he had a job to do. It was to hunt down some woman who had a deck of playing cards with a map to a fortune in jewels."

"Yeah, he found her for me. She lives above the bookstore."

"You mean, Julia Fairchild, that crazy redhead?"

"Her name was Julie Summers when I knew her a long time ago," Jimmy said. "Denny was supposed to break in the back door while I forced my way in the front, but after he fell down the stairs, I had to rethink my strategy. I'm gonna confront her tomorrow to get those cards, one way or another, but I'm not leavin' town without 'em."

"Well," Tanner said, "I gotta lock up the place right now. Then we can have a nightcap at the hotel bar, and discuss it."

A man's hand reached in the closet opening and jerked the first jacket off the hanger while Heather stood frozen to the spot. She didn't dare breathe. The closet door slid shut. For a few moments, there was silence and then total darkness.

She waited for five minutes to make sure they were gone. Then she slid the door open a crack. Stepping out of the closet, she fumbled across the dark office for the door and turned the knob.

"Locked!" She felt around the door for the lock to open it from the inside but this kind of lock needed a key, and there wasn't one in it.

Her heart sank. Then she pulled out her cell phone and texted Chad her location. She waited for an immediate reply. But there was none.

<><><>

Heather couldn't switch on the lights in case someone might notice, so she paced the floor in the dark, rubbing her thumbnail across her bottom lip until it got so sore, she had to stop.

"What's he doing? Why doesn't he text me?"

After ten of the longest minutes of her life, voices came from the hall. Heather jumped into the closet and closed the door behind her, leaving a small opening, just enough to peek out.

Someone unlocked the door and switched on the light. But she didn't hear the door close again.

"Just let me get my jacket and purse, darling," Krystal said. "Then we can leave."

Heather leaned back to get out of the way, expecting to hear Jack reply.

"I'll get them while you put the money in the safe."

That's not Jack.

The closet door slid open, and the jacket and purse were pulled from their hangers, leaving her face to face with Chad. He motioned for her to get out with a stern look in his eyes and a flick of his thumb.

As Heather slithered out of the closet, she caught a quick glimpse of the back of Krystal's head as she unlocked her father's safe. Then she tiptoed out through the open door.

Whew! I made it.

The door closed behind her. Heather sprinted down the hall, trying not to let her heels hit the floor. Once in the back room, she was able to breathe again. Anxious to get out, she swung the back door open.

An ear-piercing alarm sounded.

Chapter 33

Tanner must have turned the alarm on. Heather pulled the large, black hood over her head to cover her hair and face and ran out the door, down the alley, and headed toward the sidewalk. Before she reached it, she pulled off the hoodie and deposited it in the nearest trash can in case she was stopped. Then she hid behind it as a black and white pulled into the alley, lights flashing. Brakes screeched to a stop at the back door.

Heather sneaked around the trash can and finally made it to the sidewalk. Her hands still shook, along with her knees. Her throat was so dry, she could barely swallow. She jogged in the direction of home. What else could she do? Her car was in Chad's driveway, and his was not the best choice to get into right now, since it seemed like he was planning to drive Krystal somewhere.

After a few moments of her feet pounding the concrete sidewalk, she learned the hard way that heels weren't the best shoes to run in. By the time she got to the end of the block, her toes were throbbing. *Two blocks to go.*

Chad texted: *Where R U?*

Jogging home, she texted back, miserable that Krystal had called him *darling*. She couldn't get the two of them being together out of her thoughts.

There was no reply to her return text, so she dialed her aunt's number.

"What did you find out?" Julia asked. "We're all anxious to hear what happened."

"I found out a lot." Heather stopped running to catch her breath. "Can you get a lift home from Christine? I'm on foot."

"What happened to Chad's car?"

"I'll tell you about it later."

"Okay," Julia said. "See you at home."

Two of the longest blocks in existence and ten minutes later, Heather opened the front door of their building. Julia was right behind her, tossing a quick goodnight to Christine and running up the stairs to catch up. Heather flipped off her shoes and limped to her room to exchange them for a pair of furry house slippers.

Then she went to the kitchen and drank nearly a quart of water. It quenched her thirst but did nothing to calm her nerves.

Julia made herself some hot tea. "Do you want a cup?"

Heather flung herself down on the sofa, her insides tied in a tight little ball. "No. What I need is a drink."

"This must be bad," Julia mumbled. And a few moments later, she offered her niece two fingers of Crown Royal in a juice glass. "Sorry. This is all we have."

After a few sips to calm the tension in her stomach, Heather's insides relaxed a little.

"So, tell me what happened." Julia said.

"I think I found out who might have killed Denny," Heather said. "I believe it was Johnny Tanner. He and Denny were cellmates many years ago. That's how they knew each other. But Tanner had built a new life for himself here in Willow's Bend as Nikos' accountant at the off-track betting facility. No one here knows Tanner was in prison, and I think Denny found out he'd been embezzling money and threatened to tell Krystal."

Julia huffed. "Yeah, I can believe that. Well, at least we know who might have done it and possibly why, but how can we prove it, or at least convince the police to investigate Tanner?"

"Since I was eavesdropping on a private conversation," Heather said, "the information can't be used in court. Besides, if I said anything to Detective Lindsey, I'd be charged with breaking and entering."

"You're right about that. Did you at least find Denny's cell phone?"

"No. I think Tanner must have it. But the police will have to do a search of his place to find it. He's probably erased everything incriminating on it by now. What are we going to do?"

"I suggest you tell Chad everything tomorrow. I'm sure he'll have some ideas."

Heather paced in short, quick steps. "He really helped me get out of a tight situation tonight." She thought about texting to thank him, but if he was still with Krystal, she didn't want to give the woman a reason to be suspicious.

Just the thought of them being together put an ache in Heather's heart. *I have to concentrate on something else.*

"And speaking of tomorrow," Heather said. "Jimmy the Horse said he's going to come over and get those cards if it's the last thing he ever does. Not only that, he told Denny about the cards, and Denny told Tanner, and God only knows who Tanner told. Word seems to be spreading. I'm worried, Aunt Julia. Suppose someone else tries to get them."

"They won't if I have anything to say about it." Julia's face always took on a stern look when she meant business.

"But what I don't understand is, why does Jimmy think those cards are rightfully his?"

Julia tsked. "Sit back, finish your drink, and I'll tell you."

Heather couldn't wait to hear *this* story.

Julia sat next to her. "My grandmother called me to her home after the doctors discovered her cancer was too advanced for treatment. Jimmy came along for moral support. Unfortunately, for some reason, Gran thought we were married, so she gave the cards to Jimmy as a start for our new life together. Then she told us the story about how she got the special deck. When she worked as a nurse in a hospital in London just after the war, she cared for a young man who'd been badly injured. He was with British Intelligence attached to the Underground in Poland where his family lived. His dad had been a wealthy merchant, but when the Nazis invaded Poland, they confiscated everything. So, this young man decided to bury his mother's jewels deep in the woods near their country house, rather than let the Nazis have them."

Julia drew a deep breath. "Then he sketched out a small map so he wouldn't forget where he buried the gems. He was worried if he was captured, the Nazi's would find the map on him, so when he heard about the playing cards the soldiers in the POW camps got from the Red Cross, he got an idea. He asked one of his friends to put the map on a microdot, and then embed it on one of the playing cards, and he'd always carry the deck with him. But Gram couldn't remember which card it was."

"So you don't know?" Heather asked.

"Not for sure. But I suspect it might be the ace of spades. That's why I nearly had a heart attack when you brought that ace back and it looked almost ruined. But what's more important is that Jimmy doesn't know either. To him, it could be on any of the cards."

"Why didn't the young man go back and retrieve the jewels after the war?" Heather asked.

"He knew his injuries were too extensive, and he'd never make it, so he gave the deck to my Gran as a thank you for caring for him."

"Wouldn't those jewels rightfully belong to his family?"

"They had all died in Nazi concentration camps. A few months after the war, Gran married Gramps and immigrated to the States. She never told me what the circumstances were that prevented her from searching for the jewels, but she did say her family never had the money to visit Poland. After the war, money was tight, and Gramps was often out of a job. She kept those cards in the hopes that one day they might go to Poland together and find the jewels. But after Gramps passed away from a heart attack at such a young age, she no longer had the desire."

Julia took a sip of her tea. "She gave us the cards just before I turned Jimmy in to the FBI. That's why he wants to marry me, so he can legally get his hands on them, because he knows I'll never give them up willingly."

"I understand now. But your Gran really wanted you to have the cards, didn't she?"

"I think so, but he thinks he's entitled to them. He insists that she gave them to him. But that's not the way I remember it. No doubt, he remembers it differently."

"Why didn't you ever go after the jewels yourself?"

"I knew if I found them, I'd just squander the money. I was saving the cards as a safety net for my retirement."

Heather shook her head in disbelief. "Even if you do find the jewels, *which seems unlikely*, what makes you think the Polish government will let you keep them?"

Julia scrunched her eyes. "What makes you think I'm going to report them to the government?"

She has a point. I probably wouldn't either. "But what are you going to do about Jimmy?"

"What *can* I do?" Julia raised her eyebrows. "Guess I'll have to give him the cards, or he'll never leave me alone."

Heather could almost hear the wheels churning up a plan in her aunt's mind. *She's not going to give up those cards without a fight.*

Chapter 34

In the morning, Heather jumped out of bed well before her alarm was due to go off as a sudden thought struck her. How would she get to City Hall when her car was in Chad's driveway? She'd have to walk all six blocks. She laid her head back on the pillow, but it was useless trying to sleep with so much on her mind.

She checked the time. *Six-thirty*. She got up, showered, and even had time to wash her hair and make coffee. This was the first morning she'd been able to make herself a decent breakfast since she'd started the new job.

Julia wandered into the kitchen. "You're up early."

"Couldn't sleep. The bathroom's all yours."

After breakfast, Heather dressed, donned her walking shoes, and left early for work. The sun was shining bright this morning, and there was a mild breeze. Since she'd never had the chance to window shop in the boutiques on Main Street, this was her chance. As she approached the first store, a car pulled up next to her.

"Need a lift, lady?"

She turned at the sound of Chad's voice. He was driving *her* car.

"You bet I do."

Heather jumped into the passenger's seat. And the story of what happened last night tumbled from her lips.

Chad turned the corner and drove down the side streets. "Did you find Denny's phone?"

"It wasn't in Krystal's desk, her purse, or in the closet, but it might have been in the office safe."

"No phone in there," Chad said. "I checked. Which means Tanner might have it."

"Are you going to try to convince the police to investigate him?"

"Don't know," Chad said.

His answer wasn't exactly what Heather had expected. "What happened after I left and set off the alarm?"

Chad curled his lip in disgust. "Krystal got hysterical, her usual response to things she has no control over, and couldn't remember the code to turn it off. She had to call Tanner. Then the police looked at the video to see who set off the alarm and said it was a woman in a black hoodie. I tried to convince Krystal it was just an employee who'd stayed overtime, but she insisted we do an inventory, in case something was stolen. What a night!"

Heather scrunched her forehead. "I hope you're not angry with me for putting you in a bad situation."

Chad parked her car in front of the book store and got out. "I agreed to help. Why should I be?"

She rolled the window down and called to him. "I'll be happy to drive you and Ashley home after you close the store today."

"No worries. George Talan's bringing Ashley to the store later, and he'll pick us up at six."

"Again, I'm sorry you had to spend an unpleasant evening with Krystal."

"I'm not," he said as he walked away, the tone of his voice a little too happy for Heather's liking.

She scooted over and slipped into the driver's seat. It was still warm. This would have usually made her smile, but not today. *Last night I pushed him into Krystal's arms, and what's worse, it sounded as if he enjoyed it.*

Heather couldn't get those thoughts out of her mind as she pulled into the only empty parking space in front of City Hall and made it to her office. With her mind distracted, she unlocked her door only to find... more boxes. She could barely squeeze through to her desk. *Thanks goodness these will be gone soon.*

As the mayor had requested, she sent an email to all the departments asking them to make sure the papers they wanted shredded were in the hallway near her office early this morning, because there wasn't an inch of space *inside* her office.

She had to put up a notice in the hallway to show everyone where the boxes should be left so she typed one in Word and printed it out, but she needed tape to stick it on the wall. She checked her desk drawer and then remembered the only things there were a pen and a notepad. *Where do I get supplies around here?*

The first logical place to look was Sylvia's office. She knocked on the door and peeked in. The mayor's assistant wasn't there, so she walked in and searched the desktop. No tape. But Heather wasn't giving up. She pulled open one of the side drawers.

There were blank papers, pens, and other office supplies. She felt toward the back. Her fingers touched something metal, like a button. She pressed it, and a small hidden drawer popped open. There was a cell phone inside.

Why would Sylvia be hiding this? She picked it up. *Could this be Denny's?* Why would Sylvia have Denny's cell? She obviously knew him, since she had breakfast with him on Sunday, but why would she want to kill him and take his phone? Heather couldn't think of a motive. She turned the phone on and waited.

The lock screen requested a pin number. She turned it off. *This is silly. I'm being paranoid.* She replaced the phone in the small drawer and clicked it shut. The tape dispenser was in the larger drawer. She grabbed it and left Sylvia a post-it note message.

She barely made it back to her office door before Sylvia walked toward her with that same confident business woman's swagger she herself used when she worked in the marketing office in downtown Chicago.

"Hi, Heather. Before I forget. The shredder truck will be here in about twenty minutes to remove the boxes from your office. Sorry I didn't give you more notice, but I've been in an important meeting."

Heather nodded her recognition, passing the tape from one hand to the other in a nervous gesture.

Sylvia glanced at it. "Is that mine?"

Heather turned it over. Sylvia's name was printed on the bottom. "So it is... I mean yes, it is. I hope you don't mind. I borrowed it from your desk." Her heartbeat quickened.

Sylvia put on a fake smile like she wanted to be polite but was really miffed. "I don't mind that you borrowed the tape, but the next time you're going to rummage through my desk, let me know first. If you need office supplies, they're downstairs in the supply room next to the vending machines." A moment passed before Sylvia spoke again. "Well, I'm sure you have a lot to do with the truck coming, and I have to switch-out Marty Engels' business phone before he leaves the building this afternoon." Sylvia grinned from ear to ear. "I just heard in the meeting that today is his last day. See you later." Sylvia waved as she swaggered back to her office.

Heather let out a long breath and unlocked her door. She went in and set the tape dispenser on the desk. *That was probably Marty's other phone. And I actually thought Sylvia might be Denny's killer. This murder inquiry is making me suspicious of everyone and everything.*

She glanced at her office clock. *Oh geez.* The shredder truck would be there in ten minutes. She shouldn't have spent so much time talking.

It was nearly two in the afternoon by the time the driver finished loading all the boxes in his truck. Thankful for the extra space, Heather opened the back window and sucked in a breath of air, unpolluted by smoke this time.

Thank God it's Friday! The rest of her time was free. She couldn't do anything until the mayor approved her budget.

Chapter 35

HEATHER closed the window, grabbed her purse, locked her door, and made her way to Sylvia's office to return her tape dispenser, passing by the accountant. Marty glared at her, and Heather couldn't squelch the nagging feeling *he* might have killed Denny Serrano, but she was still looking for a motive.

Heather knocked on the side of Sylvia's open door. "I brought your tape back." She set it on the desk. "What's Marty's deal? He just gave me the iciest stare I've ever gotten in my life when I walked past his office."

"I'll tell you what I think has been going on, but we can't talk here for obvious reasons." Sylvia grabbed her purse. "It's nearly two, and I'm hungry. Aren't you?"

Heather couldn't stop her stomach from grumbling. "I am."

"Want to walk to the deli with me?"

"Sure." Heather had a few extra dollars she'd managed to save since she'd eaten lunch with Chad yesterday.

"Great," Sylvia said. "I'll order. You can pay me later. But we can't eat at the deli. We need a place to go where we can talk and not be overheard. Rumors run rampant in this town. Could we go to your apartment?"

"Okay."

Sylvia smiled. "I've always wanted to see what the flat above the bookstore looks like. I'll meet you there in about fifteen minutes."

Heather gave Sylvia her order and headed out to her car. She found it odd that Sylvia had suddenly become so chatty. Maybe it was because Marty Engels was leaving town. Or it might be because Sylvia was finally warming up to her.

She stopped at a boutique specializing in leisure wear and bought a replacement hoodie for the one she'd dumped in the trash last night.

At the apartment, Heather hurried to wash the breakfast dishes. Then she set up the card table and two chairs. She went to the kitchen to get a couple of soft drinks from the fridge as a knock sounded from the front door. She swung it open, and Sylvia sauntered in, carrying a brown paper bag.

"Wow, this place is smaller than I'd imagined."

Heather had to agree. "It *is* a bit compact. But my aunt and I are only staying for the next five months, until her community service sentence is up in November. And of course, my job at City Hall will be over too."

Sylvia set the brown bag on the card table and plopped down in one of the chairs. Her happy mood changed as her cherry-red lips frowned. "And the job I've had for the past twelve years will be gone too."

Heather was just about ask what other jobs in town Sylvia could do, when Makki pranced into the room, meowing and whipping his tail from side to side in an agitated way.

Sylvia caught her breath. "I didn't know you have a cat."

Heather picked him up. "This is Makki. He lives downstairs, but he comes up to visit sometimes." She took the cat into the kitchen and fed him a treat. He ate it, but his tail continued to swish around like he was upset about something.

"Keep him away from me," Sylvia said. "Our neighbor's tabby scratched me on the face when I was a kid, and I've never gotten over my fear of cats."

Heather couldn't imagine what Sylvia had done to the poor tabby to make it react that way. Cats weren't hostile unless they were threatened. *Makki might sense the fear in Sylvia.*

The cat crossed the living room and climbed up the bookshelf wall. It unnerved Heather that he liked to walk precariously on the ends of the shelves. And now he was standing on the very top, looking down on them.

Heather went to the kitchen and brought the soft drinks in. She handed one to Sylvia.

"So, tell me about Marty Engels.

Sylvia took a sip from her can. "I only know what I've overheard. The story around town is that he might have agreed to testify in a trial. Maybe the head of a drug cartel or someone in the mob. And the mayor made a deal with a government agency to keep Marty incognito until the trial date. But that's only rumor."

"Sometimes rumors turn out to be true." Heather grabbed her phone "And it explains a lot." She showed Sylvia the photos of the woman in green and the two men at Marty's house. "Do these people look like government agents to you?"

"When did you take these?"

"The other day on my lunch hour. Please don't tell the mayor."

"Don't worry, I won't." Sylvia checked the photos and rubbed a hand across the back of her neck. "They could be." She shrugged. "Or they could be Marty's relatives. To tell you the truth, I really don't care."

Of course she wouldn't, now that he's gone. But she hasn't convinced me those people aren't government agents. From the way Marty and the mayor have been acting lately, the rumor is probably true.

A moment later, a key turned in the lock of the front door. It opened, and a red-faced Julia flew into the living room, breathless like she'd just taken the stairs two at a time. "Where's the emergency?" She looked from one side of the room to the other.

"What are you talking about?" Heather stared at her aunt.

Julia slammed the door and leaned against it, drawing in deep breaths. "Someone from City Hall called and said there was an emergency with my niece, and I should meet her at home right away."

"You should have confirmed that with me," Heather said. "I would have told you there's no emergency. Who could have given you a ridiculous message like that?"

"Uh, that would be me." Sylvia smiled as she pulled a gun from the brown paper bag and pointed it at Julia.

Heather couldn't believe her eyes. It was like a surreal dream.

Julia folded her arms across her chest in a look of defiance and grunted. "A Sig P365 Micro Compact pistol. I haven't seen one of those in years. Denny Serrano had one." She studied the gun in Sylvia's hand. "Wait a minute. Is that Denny's pistol?"

Sylvia nodded. "How perceptive of you. I pulled it from his pocket, along with his phone, while his body was lying at the bottom of your staircase."

At this point, Heather was more confused than frightened. "Why are you doing this, Sylvia?"

"Oh, Heather, I knew you had to suspect something when I saw my tape dispenser in your hand and the nervous look on your face when you saw me. So I came up with the best excuse I could think of to get you to come home."

"You were very convincing." Heather took a few steps closer to her aunt in an attempt to reach the door. "And you were right. I did suspect you of killing Denny when I found a cell phone in your secret drawer. But I didn't know if it was his."

Sylvia smirked. "That phone has photos of me, and recent texts between us. I was going to delete them and toss the phone into the lagoon, but I don't know Denny's code to open the phone. I've been trying to figure it out for the past week."

"I still don't understand what your motive was."

Sylvia shook the gun at Heather. "How's this for a motive? Denny was going to kill me."

Heather flung her arms up in a gesture of disbelief. "Now I've heard everything. Why would he want to do that?"

"Because twenty years ago, Denny and I were lovers. He was doing small jobs for a mob boss, but he got caught dealing drugs by the police and was sent to prison for a short sentence. While he was gone, I happened to witness a murder. Just my luck. And if that wasn't bad enough, it was someone high up in the mob. As soon as I realized what I'd seen, I knew they'd have to kill me too. So I packed up and left town without telling anyone."

"You poor thing," Julia said. "You must have been terrified."

Sylvia let out a long sigh. "I was, and I didn't have much money, so I sold my car when it ran out of gas, and bought a ticket on the first train out. And that's how I ended up in Willows Bend. It wasn't much of a town then, just kind of a whistle stop. I figured no one would find me here. So I changed my name and got a job as a waitress in some dive that's long gone. I had already changed the color and style of my hair. Then, many years later, as the town grew, exponentially thanks to old Mr. Willows, I was lucky to land a job with the mayor, and later, when I could afford it, I got my nose straightened. After that, I started dating Johnny Tanner. I thought my life was set. That is, until I saw Denny in town last week, and I nearly had a panic attack."

Heather couldn't help feeling sorry for Sylvia. "But he wouldn't have recognized you, not after all you'd done to change yourself."

"That's what I thought, but he was hanging around my boyfriend, and they seemed awfully chummy. I asked Denny how he knew Johnny, and he said they'd been cell mates in prison twenty years ago. You can imagine my surprise. I didn't even know Johnny had been in prison. Anyway, I heard Denny was asking questions about me around town, so he must have suspected something."

Sylvia stopped to take a sip of Pepsi. "I knew he'd recognized my voice when he closed his eyes one day while I was talking to Johnny and then opened them with a look of shock on his face. Then, without thinking, at the restaurant Sunday morning, I added sugar to my coffee and folded my empty sugar packet into a tiny square, then set it on my saucer. He used to tease me about being so neat. That's when it dawned on me. Denny may have seen other things I did without thinking. I knew I had to kill him before he decided to turn me over to the mob. And I'm sure he would have without hesitation."

"Old habits are hard to break." Heather rubbed her thumbnail across her bottom lip. "But why didn't you just tell the police?"

Julia shook her head. "She couldn't, or they would have arrested her for being an accessory after the fact, because she didn't report the first killing twenty years ago. There's no statute of limitations on murder."

Heather couldn't see where this was going or why her aunt was being so casual about everything. "I still would have talked to the police or the FBI. After all, there were extenuating circumstances."

Sylvia waved the gun in the air. "Hey, ladies, I'm right here. Why don't you talk to me?"

"Okay," Julia said. "You obviously knew Denny well, but how did you manage to poison him?"

"That part was easy. We left the restaurant and went back to the off-track betting facility because Johnny had to open for Krystal. Denny came with us. Johnny asked if I would make coffee since no one had come in yet. And I saw my opportunity.

"Ever since Denny came to town I've been carrying around a bottle of Madam Z's Special Elixir in my purse. I'd asked her to make it up for me a few months ago, to get rid of field mice around my house. I've been waiting for a chance to use it. I missed it at the restaurant. But this was even better. No one was around to see me except Johnny, and he was busy setting up. I made the coffee extra strong, the way Denny liked it, and poured some poison in his cup. I knew he'd never taste it since he always adds four packets of sugar to his coffee. And then I added a dash of cinnamon for flavor."

She smiled. "Funny, he complimented me on the taste." A moment later, her smile faded. "Then I wiped the bottle clean and put it in Krystal's desk drawer so the police would eventually suspect *her*."

"Very clever," Heather said. "So why are you holding a gun on us? What do you want? We have no money."

"Oh, but you do..."

A vigorous knocking on the back door had everyone's head turning in that direction. Sylvia didn't look surprised. She motioned to Julia with the gun. "Open it."

Julia unlocked the door and swung it open. Johnny Tanner came barreling in. He ran up to Sylvia.

Her lips flattened as she glared at him. "Where have you been? I've been vamping here for over fifteen minutes."

He glanced at Julia and Heather without acknowledging their presence. "I just got the confirmation about Krystal selling the off-track betting place to that lawyer guy from Chicago."

"You mean, Jack Steele?" Heather asked.

Tanner waved his hand at her. "Yeah, that's the guy. But he and his fellow investors want a five-year audit of the books. Steele has already scheduled an independent firm to come in on Monday morning. I gotta get out of town before they discover I've been cookin' 'em for years."

Sylvia nodded. "We can go together, just as soon as I get those cards from Julia."

Julia crossed her arms at her waist. "What cards?"

"You know," Sylvia said. "The ones with the map of where a fortune in jewels is buried. Get them for me now, or your niece gets it right between the eyes."

"Woah!" Johnny Tanner's jaw dropped. "You didn't say nothin' about nobody gettin' killed."

"Don't worry," Julia said. "She won't pull the trigger. That would make too much noise, and she'd either be caught by the police, or I'd kill her myself."

Sylvia lowered the gun a few inches. "You're right. I don't even know how to use a gun, but I'm desperate. If the mob finds out I killed Denny Serrano and witnessed the other killing, I'm dead. I really need the money from those jewels to disappear so they won't find me."

Heather remained skeptical, having been fooled by Sylvia before. But that veil of fear in the woman's tear-filled eyes was very convincing.

"And Johnny needs to get away too," Sylvia continued. "Krystal's going to prosecute him when she finds out about the books. He promised me he was working on his gambling addiction."

Julia walked over to her purse and pulled out her deck of cards. She handed it to Sylvia. "Here. Take these. You need them more than I do. Find the map, and sell the jewels. Then, disappear. I can sympathize with you, not that I ever cooked anyone's books, but when I was in trouble, I was lucky enough to have someone come to my rescue. Consider this paying it forward."

Heather gasped. "Aunt Julia, how can you just let them go? Sylvia killed a man in cold blood, and Johnny's an embezzler."

"I feel justified under the circumstances. After all, Sherlock Holmes didn't always turn the perps over to the police."

Heather had suspected her aunt's way of looking at things was twisted, but this was just wrong. "Sherlock Holmes is fiction. This is real life. There are laws."

Julia glared at her. "Think about it. If a man was going to have you killed, wouldn't you want to kill him first? I mean, that's just self-defense in my opinion. And as far as the other... I know how addictions can make people so desperate they'll do just about anything."

Heather was mounting a rebuttal even as her aunt spoke but was interrupted by a pounding on the front door.

Chapter 36

No one in the room moved, as if they were all frozen in place.

"Who could that be?" Julia whispered to Heather.

"I hope it's not another one of *them.*" Heather motioned toward Sylvia and Tanner.

A moment later, Jimmy the Horse exploded into the room.

Heather's heart sank. *Why couldn't it be the police?*

"I should've locked the door," Julia said. "Our apartment is turning into Grand Central Station."

Jimmy glanced around. "What's everybody doing here?"

"I could ask you the same," Julia said.

"I came to get those cards. I'm tired of your evasive tactics. I won't be deterred this time."

"I suppose you're in desperate need of money too?"

"When am I not?" Jimmy glanced at Sylvia and did a double-take. "Is she holding a gun on you?"

"Yeah," Julia said. "And she's got the cards too. She and Tanner are going to Poland to find the jewels."

Tanner's nose scrunched. "Why would we want to go there?"

"Because that's where they are," Julia said. "Right, Jim?"

Jimmy eyed the cards in Sylvia's hand as if he was getting ready to snatch them away from her. "That's exactly where they are."

Tanner sauntered up to Jimmy and stood in front of him with his fists on his hips in an attempt to look tough, even though he was a foot shorter. "But Denny didn't say nothin' about having to go to Poland for the jewels."

"I didn't tell him where they were, in case he tried to double-cross me."

Tanner grunted. "He did. Denny raced up the stairs Sunday morning, trying to get here before you, so he could break in the back door and steal the cards for himself. He told me he'd been casing the joint for the past week."

Heather gasped. "You see, Aunt Julia, it wasn't evil spirits on the back landing like you thought. It was Denny Serrano."

"It may not have been spirits," Julia said. "But it *was* pure evil. Little did Denny know what was going on behind his back." She shook her head. "How ironic."

Sylvia paced the floor. "Neither Johnny nor I speak Polish. How are we going to find the jewels?" She didn't sound as if she was sorry she'd killed a man.

Jimmy gave her a Cheshire Cat grin. "Fortunately, I do speak the language. If you give me a third, we can be partners."

The mistrust in Tanner's eyes was unmistakable, but he must have realized he either didn't have a choice, or he planned to double-cross Jimmy too. "Okay, it's a deal."

His narrowed eyes met Sylvia's for a moment. She nodded as if she knew what he was planning.

Jimmy grabbed the cards from Sylvia's hand. "Let me see those. I don't trust Julia. She might have passed off any old deck as the real one."

He slipped some cards out of their age-worn box and fingered them. "They're old enough." Then he sorted through the deck until he found the ace of spades. "Okay," he said. "The ace has the correct letter and numbers on it, but why does it have all these tiny holes?"

Julia strolled over to Jimmy and glanced at the card she'd obviously done some repair work on. "Our neighbor's cat got hold of it. But I guarantee you, the cards are the real deal."

"Great!" Sylvia shouted. "Now that we have them, we gotta get outta here. But first, we have to dispose of these two."

Tanner's eyes bulged. "I'll wait for you in the car. I don't want no part of murder." He ran out the back door, his heavy shoes pounding on the steps made his intention clear.

"Coward!" Sylvia shouted after him. "And to think I was going to marry that guy."

Heather's heart beat in her ears as she ran her thumbnail over her bottom lip, waiting for some clue of what to do from her aunt.

"Ow! ow! ow!" Julia repeatedly stamped her foot on the floor.

"What's the matter with you?" Sylvia rushed over to her.

"Cramp in my foot." Julia hopped around making loud stomping noises and arousing Makki, who jumped to his feet on the top book shelf, tail pounding against the books, as if he was marking time.

"I hate when I get those," Heather said, going along with her aunt.

Finally, Julia plopped down on the sofa. She slipped off one of her walking shoes and hurled it at Sylvia's hand with such force, the gun dropped to the floor.

Heather made a dive for the pistol, but Jimmy grabbed it away from her. He took a few steps back and pointed it at all three ladies. "Clever, Julia. I knew you weren't going to give up those cards without a fight."

A flash of black flew through the air and landed on top of Jimmy's head. The cat dug his claws in, making the loudest yowling sound Heather had ever heard. He growled and scratched at Jimmy's face as the man struggled to get the cat off.

Julia stripped the gun from Jimmy's hand and tossed it to Heather.

"If you hurt that cat," Heather shouted at him, "I'll shoot you myself."

Sylvia darted to where Jimmy had dropped the deck of cards on the table, grabbed them, and sprinted out the back door. She scrambled down the stairs, as more footsteps pounded up the front steps.

Officer Henderson flung the door open and ran into the room with Chad close behind.

Heather pointed to the kitchen. "Sylvia, the mayor's assistant, is Denny's killer," she shouted. "She just ran out the back door."

But Officer Henderson just stood in the living room with his feet shoulder width apart, like a tall, brawny, sentinel. "She won't get far," he said just before pressing the call button on his two-way radio. "Stop the woman running out the back."

Then he turned to Heather. "Another officer is stationed across the street."

Jimmy continued to wrestle with Makki. "Get him off of me! Get him off!"

"Let go, Mak!" Chad ran up to them and picked the cat off of Jimmy's head, untangling his claws from the man's thinning, gray-streaked hair.

He set Makki on the floor.

The sleek feline strolled toward the kitchen as if nothing had happened, looking as calm as only a cat can. He laid on the floor and groomed himself.

Heather shoved the pistol into Officer Henderson's hand. "Here's the gun Sylvia used to threaten us. It belonged to the victim."

She went after Chad who was in the kitchen checking the cat's paws. She stooped down and gave Makki a treat.

"You saved our lives, you brave, wonderful feline." Heather kissed Makki's head and scratched under his chin.

The cat rubbed his face against her hand and purred.

"I'll have him checked out by our vet," Chad said. "*He* appears to be okay. But how are you?"

She sucked in a deep breath, not knowing what to feel. "I'm a little stunned, a little surprised at what happened, and a little shaky, but generally I'm okay."

Chad gazed at her from head to toe. "Good. I can't believe I came so close to losing you."

The concern in his voice made her warm inside, as if he'd put his arms around her. But were those only her feelings?

"You can go back to the bookstore, Chad," Officer Henderson said. "Everything's under control here."

As Chad walked out the door with Makki, Julia came into the living room with a bottle of antiseptic and a handful of bandages. She set them on the card table and went to work cleaning up the scratches on Jimmy's head while he sat in one of the chairs.

Officer Henderson took out his notebook and pen. "Tell me what happened."

Heather explained how Sylvia had gotten her to come the apartment. And then Julia gave her version of what happened after she arrived, leaving out the part Jimmy played in all this. She told the officer he was just there for a visit and happened upon a robbery taking place. She couldn't imagine what provoked the cat to attack him, unless Makki was startled when she stamped her foot on the floor.

After Jimmy was bandaged and taken to the clinic to be examined by a doctor, they went to the police station to give their official statements. On the way, Julia coached Heather about what to say, so their stories matched.

Chapter 37

HEATHER slept late Saturday morning. Their time at the police station lasted longer than she'd anticipated last night. And she only saw Chad in passing, so there wasn't an opportunity to talk.

She set a plateful of bacon in the microwave and dug out some of Makki's favorite treats. She planned to take them downstairs, as a reward, and also to give Chad the replacement hoodie she bought for him. But before she dealt with that, there were other things she had to deal with.

She grabbed a frying pan for eggs.

Julia sauntered into the kitchen and poured herself a cup of coffee. "Mmmm, bacon. I'll have a double helping."

There were a few things Heather wanted to ask her aunt about yesterday, but with so much going on, she didn't get the chance. And by the time they got home, she was so tired, she collapsed on her bed and fell into a fitful sleep.

Heather checked the microwave. "Bacon will be ready in a minute. How do you want your eggs?"

Julia glanced her way. "Scrambled... like my brain. I shouldn't have drunk so much whiskey before I went to bed last night."

Heather cooked the eggs while Julia made toast, and by the time they sat at the kitchen counter to eat breakfast, Heather was eager for some answers to calm the uneasiness she couldn't shake, about her aunt's behavior yesterday.

"Aunt Julia, why did you let Jimmy the Horse off the hook? He was going to shoot us."

Julia buttered her toast. "He couldn't, and neither could Sylvia."

Sometimes her aunt said the strangest things. "How can you be so sure?"

"Because the safety was on the gun. I spotted it as soon as Sylvia came close to me. It was Denny's pistol, and he always carried it around with the safety on."

She took a bite of toast and washed it down with a sip of coffee. "On the other hand, Jimmy never carried a gun, so I doubt if he was familiar with this one. If he pulled the trigger, nothing would have happened. Then he'd have to turn the gun around to inspect it, inadvertently releasing the safety, and would probably have shot himself. Sylvia admitted she didn't know anything about guns, so she'd most likely have done the same. Honestly, if you're going to threaten someone with a weapon, you really should learn how to use it."

A chuckle worked its way up Heather's throat. Her aunt was one of a kind. "I knew you had to be up to something because you were too casual. I thought you might have come up with a plan to have them arrested."

"I did. But I could see it wasn't going to turn out the way I figured, so I had to improvise. Actually, this proved to be much better. I owed Jimmy big time, and now I've paid him back. It's important to pay your debts."

Heather nodded. "I understand that, but really, in this case?"

"Now Jimmy won't bother me again. He'll be hot on the trail of Sylvia and Johnny Tanner if he wants those cards." Julia let out a light laugh. "I can just see them chasing each other all over Poland, if they even get that far."

"But you've lost your retirement money."

Julia munched on a piece of crisp bacon. "I might still get the cards back from the police when Sylvia and Tanner are arrested. That is, if she hasn't passed them off to someone else. But in case I don't get them back, I'll think of another way to finance my golden years. Maybe I'll get married again... but not to Jimmy."

I knew she had a contingency plan or two. "One other thing I'm curious about," Heather said. "How did the police get here so fast without being called?"

Julia pointed at Heather with a half-eaten slice of bacon. "There was something odd about the emergency call I got from City Hall. So I consulted the cards, and they told me to be careful of deceit and to use caution. That's when I made arrangements for Officer Henderson to wait downstairs in the bookstore. He told me to stomp on the floor as a signal for him to come up."

Julia's cell phone rang. She checked the caller ID and put it to her ear. "Hello, Christine." She listened for a few seconds. "Thanks. We'll be there around seven. Bye."

Heather scooped up the last of her eggs. "Where will we be around seven? You shouldn't speak for me. I might be busy later."

"The Talans are hosting an impromptu get-together at their house tonight in our honor. Just for a few friends ... and the mayor."

Heather dragged her hands over her freshly washed face. “Didn’t everyone get enough of us on the news last night? Honestly, I’m in no mood to go to a party.”

“Think of it as drinks and a free meal.” Julia took a sip of coffee. “Besides, you have to go. They’re all anxious to hear the story of what happened yesterday, straight from the horses’ mouths, so to speak. And speaking of horses …”

She picked up her phone. “I have to place a bet on the winning horse in the second race at Arlington Park this afternoon.”

“How can you be sure the horse is going to win? What happened to the evil curse?”

“I know the curse has been broken.” Julia snapped her fingers. “Because the horse’s name is Cartomancy. And the cards have never steered me wrong.”

This made no sense to Heather. How could some random playing cards assure her aunt a horse was going to win his next race? But then, stranger things had happened since they arrived in Willows Bend.

That evening, Heather knocked on the door of the Talan’s house and glanced at her aunt in amazement. Loads of cars were parked in the street in front of their home and in the driveway, along with several in the Willows’ driveway next door.

“I thought you said there were only going to be a few friends and the mayor. It looks like there’s quite a crowd here already.”

Julia popped a tiny mint into her mouth and shrugged. “That’s what Christine told me when she called.”

Heather brought the new black hoodie and a package of cat treats for Makki with her. She'd avoided Chad that morning because she had a bad feeling about what he was going to tell her, and she wanted to put it off as long as possible.

Christine opened the door. "Come in, ladies. It's so nice to see you." She closed it and whispered, "I have to confess, I was worried about you after what happened yesterday."

Heather sauntered in and spotted Krystal standing in the statuesque posture only a model, or in this case a former model, could hold for any length of time. Her waist-length, shiny black hair hung down the bare back of her cream, Dolce & Gabbana Chantilly lace dress. Heather had almost bought the same dress for Christmas last year when she was living in Chicago and could afford such an extravagance, but now she was glad she'd passed it up. Tonight, she'd chosen a simple spaghetti-strap, silk dress made by no one famous, in pale green, to offset her auburn hair and accent the color of her eyes.

Jack Steele, in his crisp white shirt and navy jacket, stood next to Krystal, looking his handsome self. This was odd. He'd never stood by *her* when he could schmooze the room for beautiful women.

When their eyes met, Jack rushed up to her, a full champagne flute in hand.

"Thanks." Heather grabbed it from him and took a gulp.

His grin was as bright as his teeth were white. "Have you heard the fantastic news?"

Heather had never seen him this happy, not even on the day he asked her to move in. "I'm not sure. I've been a little busy."

"Oh yeah, I saw you on the local news last night. You uncovered Denny Serrano's killer. So who does that make you... Miss Marple?"

The sarcastic tone in Jack's voice and his thoughtless putdowns used to distress her, but she didn't care anymore. Heather finished the champagne and placed a hand to her mouth suppressing a burp.

Jack smirked. "My news is more important. Krystal and I are going into business together." He turned to look at his new partner, who was caught up in an intense conversation with the mayor.

The admiration in Jack's eyes told Heather this was going to be a disaster. She could see the two narcissists clashing already.

"I hope you have a long and happy business relationship." *But I doubt it.*

She didn't want to tell Jack that Johnny Tanner, Krystal's accountant, had been cooking the books at the off-track betting place for years, so their partnership wasn't a done deal yet. She would let Jack find out for himself on Monday. Just knowing he'd probably break off the deal and leave town soon was good enough for her.

She handed him the empty flute. "Thanks for the drink. Excuse me, I have to find someone."

Anxious to get away, Heather glanced around the crowded room. Too many people she didn't know congratulated her, introduced themselves, and shook her hand, in too small of an area.

Heather waved her hand in front of her face to bat away all of the competing fragrances. She inched her way to where Chad stood in the corner talking to George Talan, Christine's slightly chubby, partially balding, truck driver husband.

She greeted them. “Hi.”

Chad smiled.

George nodded. “You were very brave dealing with the Serrano killer, Heather.”

She let out a slow breath. “It was a scary situation for a while. But my aunt deserves all the credit for how it turned out.”

George’s eyes flashed as he mopped the perspiration from his forehead with the back of his hand. Julia was not his favorite person. “Excuse me,” he said. “I’m going to open the sliding glass door to the yard for more room.” A moment later, he melted into the crowd, leaving her alone with Chad.

Heather held out her hand with the black hoodie along with the package of cat treats. “I forgot to return this to you.” Her eyes glanced at the floor. “And I bought Makki a reward for his meritorious service in the face of danger.”

Chad took the hoodie and the treats. “I thought Makki was only protective of my sister. Guess you come in a close second.” He eyed her dress, her face, and her hair, in that order. “You look gorgeous, tonight.”

“Thanks.” Heather didn’t know what else to say. His compliments always made her a little uncomfortable. “How *is* Makki?”

“The vet checked him out this morning, said he was okay, but he’s at home with Ashley. She didn’t want to deal with Jack and Krystal after the fiasco with dinner at the Vendeglo last week.

Heather needed to broach the subject of Chad and Krystal before any more time passed. Her nerves couldn’t take the strain. She was glad she drank that Champagne earlier. *Guess I’d better jump in.*

"I suppose Krystal told you all about her and Jack becoming business partners when you had your talk?"

"Yeah," he said. "Krystal had no idea how much work a business takes or how time consuming it would be to run. I'm glad we had that conversation the other night, because the memories of why I didn't want to marry her came flooding back. And confirmed I'd made the right decision leaving town five years ago."

Heather's spirit rose as if she'd just gulped a second glass of Champagne.

Well-dressed guests milled around the living room and nudged each other toward the center until a large crowd had gathered around the coffee table. Voices dropped to a murmur.

"What's going on over there?" Heather asked.

"It's the reason everyone's here." Christine passed them as she edged her way toward the crowd. "They're waiting for your aunt to give them card readings."

Heather couldn't help laughing from embarrassment. "How could I be so naive as to think people came here to see and talk to *me* about what happened yesterday?"

Chad gazed into her eyes, making her defenses sizzle like cold rain on a hot sidewalk. "*You're* the only one *I* came here to see. Let's sneak out and have dinner where we can be alone."

That suited Heather. "At the Blue Moon Hideaway?" she suggested in a low voice.

Chad whispered his agreement in her ear, making her smile.

Heather sighed. If she played her cards right, this could be the first of many lovely evenings with Chad in Willows Bend.

The End

Thank you for reading, *Death in the Cards*, the third book in the *Willows Bend Cozy Mysteries Series*. If you enjoyed it, please leave a review. Reviews are extremely important to authors and also to readers like you, so take a few minutes to leave a review on Amazon today. It really does make a difference.

Other Novels by Evelyn Cullet:

The Charlotte Ross Mysteries:

Love, Lies and Murder

Masterpiece of Murder

Once Upon a Crime

The Tarkington Treasure

The Willows Bend Cozy Mysteries:

You Bet Your Life: Book 1

An *Author Shout* Silver Award Winner

The Crone's Curse: Book 2

For more information, check out her website:
https://evelyncullet.com

About the Author

Evelyn Cullet has been writing since high school when she got her start with short stories. She began her first novel while attending college later in life and while working in the offices of a major soft drink company. Now, with early retirement, she finally has the chance to do what she loves best—write full time. As a life-long mystery buff, she was a former member of the Agatha Christie Society and is a current member of the National Chapter of Sisters In Crime. When she's not writing mysteries, reading them, or reviewing them, she hosts other authors and their work on her blog, https://evelyncullet.com/blog. She is also a pianist, an amateur lapidary, and an organic gardener.

www.ingramcontent.com/pod-product-compliance
Lightning Source LLC
LaVergne TN
LVHW050626100826
845148LV00011B/1744

* 9 7 9 8 2 1 8 2 2 9 9 0 0 *